DAVID, THE BIG D, AND THE
AND THE
PLAYGROUND GOLIATH

MARIA GOSSETT

WESTBOW
PRESS®
A DIVISION OF THOMAS NELSON
& ZONDERVAN

WestBow Press books may be ordered through booksellers or by contacting:

WestBow Press
A Division of Thomas Nelson & Zondervan
1663 Liberty Drive
Bloomington, IN 47403
www.westbowpress.com
844-714-3454

Scripture quotations taken from The Holy Bible, New International Version® NIV® Copyright © 1973 1978 1984 2011 by Biblica, Inc. TM. Used by permission. All rights reserved worldwide.

ISBN: 979-8-3850-3591-5 (sc)
ISBN: 979-8-3850-3592-2 (hc)
ISBN: 979-8-3850-3593-9 (e)

Library of Congress Control Number: 2024921495

Print information available on the last page.

WestBow Press rev. date: 11/30/2024

CHAPTER

MY GREAT BIG D LIFE

I WALKED THREE quarters of a mile to Hunger Heights Middle School every morning. It was like walking through a field with hungry vultures above me and coyotes behind every bush. I tried to leave early before they caught up to me. The Hunger Heights Mafia thought they owned everything around here, so they thought they owned me.

I was short and skinny with red hair and a cowlick that wouldn't give up popping up even if I plastered it down with Kelley's super glue hair mousse. I considered myself a geek. In my old school, I liked being a geek. All my friends were geeks too. I had not met another geek like me at Hunger Heights Middle School. There were just jocks and bullies and wannabe jocks and bullies.

So I was by myself a lot. That made me a target for them, Rayjohn Roybell, Mick Keller, and Jackson Smyth. Unfortunately, they also lived in the apartments.

I heard them coming up behind me, growling like a pack of thirsty coyotes smelling blood—mine! They were laughing, not *ha ha funny* but *ha ha, what are we gonna do to Davy next?* I walked faster. I didn't want to run. That would show I was scared, which I was. If I could just get to the schoolyard where there were more kids. Not that it mattered. These kids liked watching other kids get bullied. Just off the playground, behind the bushes, they would make a circle around the bully and the victim of the day. It was entertainment to see a poor kid get beat up. That's why the Mafia ruled the school!

"Hey, you. Yeah, you, little Davy. You know what to do," said Rayjohn in his raspy cigarette-smoking voice. He was two feet behind me. I turned to face him, straightened my back, looked up at his fat, pimply face, and smiled so wide my jaw hurt.

"Got anything good in that backpack? What did the old lady pack you for lunch?"

I slipped my backpack to the ground, bent down, opened it, and took out the brown paper sack. I handed it to Rayjohn, who looked inside, sniffed, and frowned.

"Can't she do any better than PB and J? Tell her you want bologna with deli mustard tomorrow. But we'll take the bag of chips and the Little Debbie cupcakes. Put those on her shopping list too. Here, guys, a snack before school." He tossed a pink cupcake pack to Mick and a small bag of potato chips to Jackson, then pointed his finger at me. "Tomorrow, we want more goodies, Davy!"

2

CHAPTER

MAKING THE ROUNDS AT FOOD CIRCUS

MY MOM PUT five dollars and some food stamps in an envelope that once held our electric bill. She wrote on the blank side of the envelope, "Milk, bread, cupcakes, beef ramen noodles, small bag of baby carrots, ice cream (coffee, please)."

"Mom, can I get some more chips for lunch and some bologna instead of PB and J? Oh, and some deli mustard?"

"You'll have to decide other things to leave off the list. Your father hasn't paid child support yet." Her voice was angry. I did not want to hear that.

She squished her cigarette into an empty coffee cup and handed me the envelope.

"Keep this in a safe place, David. And walk down Watson Drive to the Food Circus. Be careful and watch out."

I tucked the envelope under the waistband of my jeans and tightened my belt. The Mafia would have a hard time finding it on me.

I walked past the basketball court at the entrance to the apartments. I guess I wasn't 100 percent geek, because even though I was small, I got picked for teams at my old school.

I wished I could shoot baskets all day. I was point guard on the team at my old middle school. We were a good team. My best friend, Buddy, was the star player. He was almost six feet tall the last time I saw him, but I hadn't seen him since Mom, Kelley, and I moved out of our house. He is probably taller by now. Someday he'll play in the NBA.

Mom said we were in the time of our growth spurts. I hadn't hit mine yet. I thought moving had stunted my growth and made me lose weight. It didn't help that I didn't get to eat lunch unless I had PB and J. Rayjohn had a peanut allergy.

I passed the basketball court, and it was empty. If the Mafia were not there when I got back from the store, I could shoot some baskets. I walked faster. I wanted to get to the court before it got dark.

Leafy trees lined Watson Drive on both sides. Their green leaves were turning to red, gold, and orange, and sunlight passed through the spaces where many leaves had fallen to the sidewalk. It felt warm on my back, and I felt safe on Watson Drive.

A loud motor came up fast behind me. An odd black motorcycle with three wheels rushed past on the road, over the speed limit for sure. I couldn't see the driver, just a black helmet hunched over the handles, like there wasn't even a person, just a machine. It became a dark blur that got smaller as it sped down the hill and finally turned into a single black dot.

Cool. Someday I'd have one of those, but the two-wheel kind.

The store was crowded. It was Friday and a three-day weekend for Labor Day. I found a cart and took the envelope from the waistband of my jeans. I looked at the list.

Ice cream? What were you thinking, Mom? It's still seventy-five degrees outside. By the time I get home, you won't have coffee ice cream—maybe a lukewarm pot of coffee instead.

I pushed the cart up and down the aisles of Food Circus looking for items on the list. I found the ramen noodles in the soup aisle, but had to reach up high on my toes to get to the beef kind. l grabbed two small boxes and accidentally knocked two others to the floor. When I bent down to pick them up, a small wheel nearly rolled over my hand. Then I heard a crunch. Lucky it wasn't my hand!

"Hit and run! Clean up on aisle 10," blasted a voice over the loud speaker.

3
C H A P T E R

WHEN YOU GOTTA GO...

WHEN I LOOKED up, I saw the back of a tiny woman pushing a cart. She wore black pants and a black shirt and had the whitest hair I'd ever seen, like mounds of whipped cream piled on her head.

I got the ice cream last. I couldn't find coffee ice cream in the front of the freezer. My hands grew icicles from going all the way back, when I found a box of mocha fudge, the same color as coffee. I could live with that. I hoped Mom would understand.

Then I got in a long line. The ice cream started to sweat and so did I. Finally, the line went down to two carts. In the cart ahead of me, a little boy in the kiddie seat stared at me, creeping me out. I was getting tired of standing in line.

"Where's your mommy?" he asked.

"I am my mommy."

He smirked at me and whined to his mother.

David, the Big D, and the Playground Goliath

"Mama, Mama, I want some Gooey Gushers." He pointed to the candy shelf by the cashier as she reached for a small green pack. "No, no, I want 'ellow." She took a yellow one and handed it to him. He whined again so she grabbed the pack and opened it. He put a handful of Gushers in his mouth and grinned at me. Yellow saliva dripped down his chin.

Was I ever like that?

We waited. I was still third in line. We waited some more. There were still a ton of groceries on the counter. The cashier looked puzzled. Then another cashier came. They looked at the small pieces of paper and sorted them into two piles. A lady with white hair stood by the counter, taking more pieces of wrinkled paper out of her purse. She gave them to the cashiers who inspected each one, reading some fine print, I guessed. The lady with the whipped cream hair kept pulling them out of her purse like a magician pulling an endless supply of rabbits out of a hat.

The mother of the kid in front of me moved out of our line and went to the end of an even longer line. "Coupons!" She shook her head. "How rude!"

I was next. I loaded my groceries on the end of the belt on the counter as the woman was still taking coupons out of her purse. And then I knew for sure I had to pee—soon!

All the other lines were three or four carts deep. There was a real possibility that any second I could wet my pants. I went up to the white-haired lady, who was maybe an inch taller than me.

"Ma'am, I need help!"

She scowled at me over the black frame of her eyeglasses.

"Just a minute! I'm counting."

"I have ice cream!" I shouted. "And I have to pee—bad!"

I took the envelope, put it on top of my groceries on the counter, and ran to the bathroom.

4

SPIDER ON STEROIDS

WHEN I GOT back to the checkout counter, the lady was gone; so were my groceries and the money. I was dizzy! I walked around the crowded store in a daze. I didn't know what to do.

Outside, the Food Circus parking lot was full. I looked up and down all the rows of cars, but I did not see the woman. So I walked home slowly uphill on Watson Drive. It was my fault. I should have used the bathroom before I got in line. My feet shuffled the leaves on the sidewalk as my brain shuffled words to tell my mom.

The gate to the apartment was always open. It never closed all the way even though they called this a gated community. All the bad guys were inside the gate anyway. The sky was glowing orange, yellow, and red. Cars were parked on the street alongside the basketball court, and people were sitting on the ground or standing around the court. They watched as three Mafia guys and two other kids played a game against another team.

Shouts and cheers came from the crowd as Rayjohn slammed the ball into the rusty hoop. I wanted to play so bad. A loud motor noise sounded over the game noise as a big black three- wheeled motorcycle whizzed past the court. The action stopped for a few seconds as people looked toward the street. The coach blew a whistle and shouted, "Get focused guys! Game on!"

I watched for a while. The Mafia made some moves that should have been called if the referees were any good and honest. I knew they would probably win because they were bigger and meaner than the other team. But I had to face my mom without the groceries, so I walked slowly past two buildings and turned right on Brewster Circle. Then I saw it and caught my breath!

It was gigantic and as dark as the shadow it made on the ground. A super giant spider, black widow on steroids, was parked by the curb outside my building. I shivered. I hated spiders, and this was the biggest one I'd ever seen!

The double doors to the building opened and my older sister Kelley raced down the steps wearing her purple and gold cheerleading outfit.

"Wow, that is some rig for an old lady," she shouted. "I gotta look closer!"

"Kelley, look out! It's a spider. It's big. It can kill you. It can kill everyone in the whole apartment building!"

"Ha ha, watch me sit in it." She lowered herself onto the plush covered seat and swung her legs into the cock pit.

"You'll get in trouble," I shouted as I walked toward two rear wheels that jutted out on cable-like legs. I thought I might have to rescue my sister.

"She said I could get in it. She's pretty nice for an old lady." Kelley had her hands on the steering wheel. "I wish I could drive this. The cheering squad would love it. There's even a seat that comes out of the side if I press a button.

She is old but she's kinda pretty and cool. She and mom are inside talking and eating watery ice cream."

Kelley climbed out of the cockpit, turned, walked past me and waved, "See you later after cheerleading practice! Go on, you know you want to get in there. See what the inside of a spider feels like!"

I wasn't brave like Kelley. I didn't even want to go inside my apartment. Then I heard mom call me from the open window.

"Davy, come on in. I want you to meet someone."

5

CHAPTER

AURORA

I OPENED THE door and a white cloud of hair rose up from the sofa facing the window. It was the woman ahead of me in line at the Food Circus. Heat came up my neck and covered my face. When she turned toward me my skin must have been the same color as my red hair.

"Aurora, this is my son, David," said my mom.

My knees started to shake.

"I believe that we have already met." The corners of her mouth lifted into a wide grin. Her teeth were big and as white as her hair. That seemed to make her skin darker than I remembered.

"David, your manners," Mom frowned.

"Nice to meet you, ma'am." I looked down at the grease spot on the worn out rug. Then I looked up at my mother who was probably smoking her fiftieth cigarette.

Did I tell you my voice is doing strange things? It goes high and then low, especially when I'm nervous.

"You can call me Aurora, David. A ROAR A." Her voice got louder on the middle syllable. "Your mother says you are a big help to her. I thought it so sweet that you do the grocery shopping." She smiled.

Mom grinned while I squirmed.

"I told your mother that I could use a responsible young man to help me with chores around my house. This week I need someone to rake and bag the leaves in my yard. I live off of Watson Drive, just up the hill. And I will pay you $10.00 for every hour you work."

Mom focused her eyes on me as if I had been awarded the jackpot on her favorite game show, The Price Is Right. She was waiting for me to race up to the stage and claim my prize, a rake!

"Davy, what do you say? This nice lady has offered you a paying job. You'll be helping out the family. And you could buy some stuff for yourself!"

"Yeah, I guess so." *Did I have a choice?*

The lady smiled and clapped her hands. Some bright red lipstick caught on her teeth. She stood up to a height of 4'10," I'd guess. She picked up the black helmet that was beside her on the sofa.

"Then I will see you this Saturday at 9AM sharp. I will have a rake and bags ready for you. Your mother has my address and phone number."

She put on the helmet that covered her whole head. She looked like a tiny Darth Vader. "Au Revoir," in a muffled voice came through the mouth piece.

We watched at the window as she slid behind the wheel of the spider and took off. I was sure everyone noticed, including the Mafia.

"What is "aw river, anyway?" I asked mom.

"I think it means 'good bye' in French," she shrugged. "What a lovely name, Aurora. Isn't she sweet?"

"I guess," I shrugged.

6
CHAPTER

A GAME OF
BASKETBALL

MOM WASN'T MAD at all. In fact, I hadn't seen her so happy in a long time.

"She told me what happened at Food Circus, David. She saw the envelope that had our address on it. The ice cream was starting to melt while you were in the restroom so she decided to deliver the food on her way home. She lives in one of those mansions up the hill. What a lucky thing for all of us!"

I wasn't so sure. She may be little, but she's scary to me, not to mention the strange motorcycle that up close looked like a gigantic live spider.

"Can you believe she's eighty years old? I won't make it that far, but I hope I'm like her when I get older."

I couldn't help myself. "I'm sure she doesn't smoke or drink beer," I said.

"She had a lot of fruit and vegetables in her cart," I added softly while mom opened another pack of cigarettes.

She looked at me, her eyes a sad shade of blue.

"I wish I could give up smoking. I know it's not good for me."

I walked behind the chair, put my arms around her shoulders, and kissed the top of her head.

"I love you, Mom. I'm going over to the court to shoot some baskets."

"Dinner in one hour. If that gang of thugs is there, come right home!"

I dribbled the basketball and practiced some turns as I danced my way to the court.

Having a job and making money for myself could be very good. Maybe I could make enough to pay the extra rent so Doug could live with us. I hope Doug is OK.

The basketball game was over. The Mafia probably won. They don't have as much skill as the team at my old school. They have size and strength, bully strength.

Good, the court was empty. I ran and dribbled the ball from one goal to the other and slam dunked it into the baskets. I did this about ten times. Each time I was faster.

The setting sun left enough light for me to take a few shots from the foul line. This is hard with no one to get the ball, but I wanted to practice this skill. I missed Buddy. We used to practice everyday after school at my old house. Dad put a basketball goal in the driveway. I wish I could go there and play with Buddy again. Wonder how the team is doing?

"Well, looky here. Little Davy can play round ball. Too bad he's too short for our team, right boys?" His voice punched me in my ears.

They came at me out of the orange and yellow sunset. I squinted and looked up to see Rayjohn, Mick, and Jackson.

"He's small enough to fit through the basket. What do you think? Let's play some three on one, and Davy can be the basketball."

Rayjohn laughed and lunged at me. His face was red and mean. His upper arms were at my eye level. They were as thick as my waist. When I looked up I saw his gray eyes bulging out of their sockets.

As he reached down to grab my arm I went into automatic pilot mode. Propelled by some force inside me, I dribbled the ball, guiding it between the legs of Rayjohn and Mick. I skirted past Jackson and ran off the court and onto the field. Turning quickly I hurled the ball and hit Mick in the stomach. He went down and shouted a cuss word in my direction.

Did I really do that? Didn't mean to hurt him. It happened so fast I didn't think about what I was doing.

I ran after the ball, got it, and sprinted across the court to the street. People were driving home from work, so I skirted between cars as horns honked behind me. I turned into my street and saw them walking off the field. Mick was still hunched over between Jackson and Rayjohn.

"You'll pay for this, Davy!" Rayjohn lifted his arm and shook his fist at me.

7

CHAPTER

WHAT'S FOR DINNER, MOM?

"I SAID ONE hour and you are right on time." Mom squished her cigarette into an ash tray and got up from the couch. "Dinner for two tonight. Kelley went for pizza with her cheerleading friends."

I pictured a large crusty pepperoni pizza, cheese dripping on the plate. I could almost smell it, and my mouth watered.

"Help yourself," Mom handed me a plate and pointed to a big pot on the stove. I used a serving spoon to scoop out ramen noodles with some vegetables and pieces of leftover chicken.

"One pot meal! All the food groups are in one place. Easy peasy," she said, as she poured me a glass of milk. "Ice cream for dessert, mocha fudge. What happened to the coffee?"

"They were out of coffee, Mom."

"Well, mocha fudge will do. Hope it's solid now. It was a bit runny when Aurora and I tried some." She twisted ramen noodles around her fork. "Bon Appetite. Aurora has gotten me into French again. I took it in high school."

That name again!

"Oh yes, she wants you to work Saturday from nine to noon. That's thirty bucks! And she wants to feed you lunch. Of course her lunch couldn't compare to this spread."

My mother was once a good cook. BD (before divorce) she did a home cooked meal every night. I loved her spaghetti and meatballs, lasagne, pork chops, Tuesday taco night! The big D changed everything. I once had a happy mom who hugged me and smelled like rose perfume, not cigarette smoke.

I don't know who wanted this divorce thing. Well, I do know. It was Dad. I hate him! No, I don't, I love him! He is very tall. I guess I get my short height from Mom. Maybe that's why he likes Kelley better. She is more like him, tall, popular.

Dad was a salesman. He could sell you an igloo if you lived in Florida. He'd probably tell you how much you'd save on air conditioning. And he'd say some numbers real quick, hand you a paper and pen, tell you to sign on the bottom line.

He was so good at his job that we lived in a nice big house. I had my own room and even my own bathroom. Now I have to get through all of Kelley's girly stuff to brush my teeth in the bathroom sink.

Mom says this apartment is only for a little while. She is applying for teaching jobs, but so far she hasn't heard from any schools. I worry that she needs to take better care of herself because she is so thin and her hair is not pretty the way it used to be.

She says she can't afford to get her hair or nails done anymore. When I get paid, I'll make sure she goes to the beauty salon every week. Aurora's job offer was sounding better and better.

8
CHAPTER

FIRST DAY ON THE JOB

"YOU ARE RIGHT on time, David." The heavy wooden front door groaned as she pushed it open. She looked like a little girl with white hair standing in the humongous doorway of a castle. I wondered that if I entered this house would I get smaller too, and would I ever come out? That scared me!

"Come in, come in. Don't be shy. I don't bite, nor do I have any hungry creatures lurking in closets waiting for their dinner. Hee, Hee, Hee!"

Her cackling laugh and toothy smile made me shiver.

How badly do I need this job?

Before I could turn and run I felt her arm circle my shoulder, grip my upper arm, and push me through the castle door. It shut slowly behind us with the same painful groan.

I'm never getting out of here!

I was surrounded by dark and shadowy outlines of big objects which became stuffed chairs, sofas, and heavy wooden end tables as my eyes adjusted. The room smelled old. I had entered a house for old people. I was scared of old people. I was scared of this strange old woman.

She flipped a switch on the wall near the door. Four large umbrella-shaped glass bowls hung from the ceiling, each containing ten or so small light bulbs. It was an army of lightbulbs overhead that lit up the room.

I could see that every part of the room held glittering treasures. Small shiny statues and crystal glassware sat on carved wood tables. Colorful rugs with pretty patterns covered parts of the old wood floors. The chairs and sofas were upholstered in gold and red velvet. My mom would love this place. It was like the antique stores she would drag me to before we got poor.

"David, you can call me Ahh ROAR Ahh." Again she accented the ROAR. I felt uncomfortable.

"Here is your list of chores." She handed me a notecard with neatly printed and numbered tasks.

1. rake leaves in front yard
2. put leaves in lawn bags
3. put lawn bags by the curb
4. repeat for back yard
5. don't get close to shed
6. come inside the back door and wash up in bathroom
7. join me for lunch in the main dining room. (Just follow the aroma of the baking bread)

"Any questions? No? Then you'd better get started."
She took my arm and led me out the front door to the wide

porch. She pointed toward a tall oak that was shedding leaves in the breeze.

"Your tools for the task, my dear David."

I saw a rake, the kind that looks like a fan at the bottom, leaning against the trunk of the tree. Beside it on a metal bench was a box of lawn bags.

"Au revoir," she said as she turned. "Petite dejeuner at noon. I will ring the bell." Aurora disappeared inside the door.

I guessed that meant lunch at noon. I felt scared at the idea of eating lunch alone with her in that big old house.

The rake was light. I got down to business, glad that the wind was calm. Soon I had collected an impressive pile of leaves.

I cleared another area of lawn that had six big trees and a ton of leaves on the ground, and I moved them into another neat pile. I liked raking and gathering the leaves, but I didn't feel like bending down to stuff them into bags.

9
CHAPTER

FRIENDLY NEIGHBOR

"CAN I JUMP in the leaves?"

A neighbor kid had been watching me. He was about five or six years old with a sturdy build, wide dark eyes, and dark hair. He was wearing a red sweatshirt with a faded team logo. Then I had an idea.

"Ok, but if you do three jumps you have to fill one trash bag with leaves. Then you can jump three more times."

"Do you know the lady who lives here?" I asked him.

He shook his head and made an ugly face.

"My mom told me to stay away. She says that lady is strange. She has a big black scary bike that makes a lot of noise."

The kid was good at stuffing bags. I figured he would do two or three bags before he got bored. He did. We worked about half an hour.

I went to the bench to get another bag. Two icy cold juice

boxes were on the bench with a note. "Good job, boys, merci." The fruity drinks tasted good. I said, "Merci," to the kid who was ready to go home. "That means thank you in French, I think."

I filled three more large black lawn bags and dragged them across the grass to the curb. The seven stuffed bags stood at attention, like palace guards. The front yard looked clean. I felt pretty good.

I hope these drinks aren't poisoned. I'm scared to have lunch with her. I might never come back out. She seems nice, but a lot of bad people seem nice at first.

I grabbed the rake and bags and headed to the back of the house. The back yard was as big as the front. It had the same number of trees scattered around. One had a tire swing attached by a thick rope to a solid looking branch. I love a tire swing. Maybe when I finished up, I would try it.

I started raking far away from the shed. It was made of rusty metal, and looked to be about the size of my room in the apartment. There was a door in the front with a lock. I could see a window on one side. It was a plain old metal shed where there might be a lawn mower inside, the kind you ride.

Maybe I'll get to mow the lawn if she hires me again. Or, there could be other things inside like live things, scary things. There could be cages where she keeps little kids.

She said not to go near it, so I didn't, but I had to get closer to rake all the leaves.

I filled four more bags and twisted wire ties around the tops. I dragged them to the front where they joined the line up by the curb. There was one large oak tree near the shed, and bushes and weeds were all around it. That was the last thing I needed to do. I gathered them into a pile, and thought I'd have a chance to look into the window of the shed.

I creeped up, not too close, maybe three feet. The window was covered on the inside by a dark curtain. It was quiet and still around the shed. I only heard the sound of weeds crunching under my feet, then a soft hum, the steady low buzz of insects coming toward me. I stuffed leaves into the bag and ran to the curb clutching the bag to my chest. I looked back to see if anything was following me. The swarm had turned another direction.

I remembered my promise to myself, to try out the tire swing. I think it had been a long time since someone used it. Moss grew inside the rubber tire and on the ropes. But it looked like it could hold me just for one or two swings. I slipped my body through the center, sat on the rubber rim, then pumped my legs and held on. I felt so free as I got higher and higher off the ground.

I heard the bell, a deep important bell, like a church bell, and I heard her call my name." David!"

10
C H A P T E R

GRACE

AURORA STOOD ON the back porch wearing a white apron and a hat, like the chefs wear in fancy restaurants. She was ringing a bell which hung by a rope from the roof of the porch.

"Ah, David, I have been watching you work. You do a good job, and you were clever to get that little one to help you. I am glad you discovered the tire swing. No one has used it since, well," her voice trailed off. "Never mind, come in," she said in a stronger voice.

She led me inside the back door and I followed her down a hallway with doors on either side. She pointed to one on the right.

"Here is a restroom, David. You need to wash for lunch. Don't be long. The bread is almost done, and cheese is melting on the soup. When you're cleaned up, just follow the scent of baking bread to the dining room."

The room was white and clean. I washed all the dirty parts of me. I took a small towel from a stack on the counter and wiped my face, arms and hands. It turned light brown from all the sweat and dirt. I folded it and set it by the sink.

My stomach complained. It was hungry. It grumbled and growled as I followed the salty, sweet smell. It reminded me of the bakery in the town where I used to live. When I was real little my mom shopped there, and the owner always gave me a fresh baked cookie. Mom would buy a loaf of bread and crumb cake, Dad's favorite.

Aurora stood by a round table in the middle of a room which was lit by another glass upside down bowl hanging by a thick gold chain from the ceiling. She pulled a metal cord and soft light came through the glass making blue, red, and yellow patterns on the table cloth. Two swans stood on plates facing each other on the table. They were just white cloth napkins folded in a certain way.

Fancy French restaurant. I wish mom were here. What's on the menu? Snails, snakes, octopus?

Aurora pulled out one of two chairs. "Please sit down, David."

The chair seat was puffy and covered in faded red velvet. I sank into it. She was still dressed like a cook or server, and she held a pitcher in her hand.

"You must be thirsty." She poured water into a glass in front of me already filled with ice and a slice of lemon.

"Taste!" She ordered.

It was like lemonade, but not so sweet. I drank the whole glass, and she poured more. I was so thirsty I didn't think that it might be poison.

She disappeared through a door probably leading to the kitchen. A minute later she came out with a tray holding two bowls. She placed one steaming bowl on the plate in front of me. Melted cheese bubbled up like tiny white balloons then burst and slid down the side of the bowl to form little puddles that turned into goo on the plate.

"Wait and let it cool and calm down inside."

What needs to calm down inside? French people eat funny things like rats and snails and fingers and toes of little kids.

"It's French onion soup with a bit of meat, for protein."

Meat? I didn't dare ask? I'll just leave it in the bowl. I can live on bread. I couldn't wait to get my teeth into the loaf in front of me on the table.

"While we're waiting for the soup to cool we can say Grace."

Say what? We don't do that in my family. One Thanksgiving before we ate Dad said, "Ok, let's all hold hands and bow our heads." Kelley and I rolled our eyes at each other. But we all reached around the table and grabbed hands. Dad's grip was tight on my small child's hand. Kelley's hand felt soft and warm.

"God is great, God is fine, thank you for this food and wine, now DIG IN!"

He had a lot of God's good wine that night, and Mom did too. They had a fight in the kitchen about cleaning up the mess. I would have done it, but I was too small. Kelley did some of the dishes. I went upstairs and crawled into bed. Doug followed me and slept beside me, my best friend. I had to hold back tears, I missed him so much!

11

CHAPTER

CHOCOLATE MOUSE

AURORA CLASPED HER hands together on her lap and bowed her head. I did the same.

"Dear father God," she said.

"Dear father, " I started to say.

Then I caught her stern look from across the table.

"Just listen to what I say."

"Sorry," I whispered.

"Father God, I thank you for bringing David here today to help me. You know I need help with things since my Louis died. And you know I need someone to cook for every now and then.

God, you are good to me. Thank you for giving me the strength to cook this food, the money to buy the food, and David to share the food with me. Amen"

"You can say 'Amen,' David."

"Amen David," I said.

She laughed. I guessed she found something about that amusing.

I dug my spoon through the layer of cheese into the warm liquid until it hit some solid pieces.

"Ma'am, I don't mean to be rude but what's in this soup? I have allergies."

She smiled. "It is beef my dear. I bought it at Food Circus yesterday. The soup also has onion, lots of onion, some carrots for color and kale for vitamins, and quite a bit of cheese that came from France. It has some secret spices because it is French. That's all I can say."

"I think it will be all right." I put a spoonful in my mouth. It tasted every bit as good as it smelled. I broke off a large piece of bread and spread butter over it. The crust was crunchy and chewy and the inside soft and squishy. I had two helpings of soup, and another big piece of bread.

While I ate Aurora spoke about France. I learned that in France people take two hours to eat lunch. Then they have a small meal when they finish work at six o'clock. French people like good, fresh, slow food.

"Oui, we do have McDonald's in France. We call it MacDo. In Paris they are nice cafes where you can get croissants and other pastries. You can get your burgers too, but better," she winked.

When we finished eating Aurora stood up and started clearing the dishes. She placed them on a large tray and carried it into the kitchen.

"Time for dessert!" She turned her head around and smiled.

Oh no, I couldn't fit any more in my stomach.

She came out of the kitchen with two glass bowls full of chocolate pudding each topped with whipped cream and a cherry.

"There is always room in the tummy for mousse au chocolat."

She placed a bowl in front of me. It looked like chocolate, smelled like chocolate, but she said it was 'moose'.

"Ma'am, I have to know if there is moose meat in this bowl. I'm allergic, remember."

Again, I didn't think I said anything funny, but she did.

"Mousse is spelled m-o-u-s-s-e, not m-o-o-s-e or m-o-u-s-e. It is like pudding, only much more delicious."

She was right. It was dark and sweet and silky smooth. I could have eaten it all day.

"I will give you some to take home to your mother. But I must have the container back next week."

When she returned to the kitchen with the empty bowls, I looked around the room. Paintings of old time people in old time clothes hung on the walls They were of different sizes, but all were framed in gold painted wood carved with swirly designs. Some of the people in the paintings reminded me of Aurora. I wondered if she actually lived in all those different times. She could be a time traveler. Anything was possible.

"These paintings are of my family. As you can see my roots go back in time, to France, of course."

She handed me three ten dollar bills and a five and led me to the front door. I put the money in the waistband of my jeans.

"This is for your family to enjoy." She gave me a shopping bag from Food Circus filled with containers of leftovers.

"I will see you next Saturday at 9 o'clock sharp! Au revoir, David."

"Aw river, and thank you, ma'am."

12
CHAPTER

COMPLIMENTS TO THE CHEF

MY AFTERNOON SHADOW walked ahead of me, long and thin, like I wished I were. I followed it past the mansions on Watson Drive. Further down the hill, the big houses turned into small ranch homes with kids' toys in the yards and barking dogs behind fences.

I heard cheers and shouts again as I got to the gate of Hunger Heights Apartments. People sat in lawn chairs or on blankets on the grass around the basketball court. The Hunger Heights Mafia was up against some bigger guys this time.

I stopped to watch at the center line. Hunger Heights had possession. They had only one strategy and that was to pass the ball to Rayjohn as soon as he got close enough to the basket to score. He was the only one on that team allowed to shoot, and he never missed as long as he was playing against little guys. Sure enough, Mick passed to Rayjohn who was to the left of the goal in a perfect position to score.

From across the court, in a familiar purple shirt, number eight charged ahead and knocked the ball out of Rayjohn's hands.

"Yeah, Buddy. You got it, man!" The Mafia didn't stand a chance against my old team and my best friend Buddy. Once they got possession they scored easily. I stuck around until they had a healthy lead.

I ran the rest of the way home singing "Hallelujah, Hallelujah," like it was Christmas! What a good day! What a perfect day! I opened the front door, excited to give Mom the money I'd earned and the great dinner I was bringing with me.

"Mom, I'm home. Aurora gave me $35.00 and some really good food. Mom, where are you?" The TV was on in her bedroom. She was watching some game show where people got excited and the audience applauded, yelled, and took sides.

She was still in her PJ's sitting on the bed. Cigarette smoke formed patterns in the sun streaming in from the window.

"That's good, Dave." She smiled and held her hand out for the money. She counted it, then handed me the five dollar bill.

"This is for you. Save it or spend it."

"Thanks, Mom. Aurora wants me back next Saturday. She has a lot of jobs for me. She packed some leftovers, too, so you don't have to cook tonight."

"That is so sweet of her. I am too tired to cook. Are you still afraid of her, Dave?"

"I don't know. She's been real nice to me but—"

But what? I kept thinking about that story, the one about the brother and sister who got lost in the woods. They see a gingerbread cottage. And a sweet old lady invites them in to eat all these good things, pizza, ice cream, cookies, all the foods kids like. They eat so much that they fall asleep. When they wake up they are locked in cages. The lady is really evil and feeds them to make them fat, so she can cook them in a crock pot. Hansel and Gretel, that's their names!

"But what, David?"

"But the food is real good, especially the chocolate mousse. Maybe she'll give you the recipe. I put the stuff in the refrigerator, Mom. Just stick it in the microwave, except for the mousse. It's like pudding and has to stay cool. I'm gonna go shoot some baskets."

"Be careful! I don't trust the gang that hangs out there."

CHAPTER

BULLIES AND BONES

THE GAME WAS over. I think the high school won. Two guys were on the court, but they weren't shooting baskets. Buddy had his hands on his hips and stood two feet from Rayjohn who was clenching his fists toward Buddy. I couldn't hear what they were saying, but it didn't look friendly. I moved closer and hid behind a dumpster.

It sounded like Buddy was trying to get Rayjohn to let the high school team have time to practice on the court and schedule some games there. The outdoor court at the high school was off limits for the season because of damage.

Good luck, Buddy. The Mafia thinks they own the court and every thing else in Hunger Heights.

When Buddy starts to get mad his voice cracks like mine. He shouted, "That's ridiculous! You don't own this place. The apartment management company has already given the school permission to use the court."

"Yeah, well they didn't ask me." Rayjohn puffed up his chest and moved closer to Buddy. " The boys and I, we run this place. If you want to play ball here it will cost you, a lot!"

Buddy's face was burning red. He moved toward Rayjohn. I came out from behind the dumpster and calmly dribbled the ball toward them. Rayjohn was a second away from punching Buddy.

"Hey guys, what's up?"

"Get lost little Davy. Not your business."

"Buddy's my best friend!" I rushed in between them and grabbed Rayjohn's legs. He didn't expect that. And I didn't expect that he would break loose, step on my arm, and slam his fist into Buddy's right cheek.

"You don't mess with my best friend!" Buddy grabbed Rayjohn's two arms and locked them behind his back.

The pain in my right arm felt like a dentist was drilling into the bone. I tried to lift it in an effort to stand. Between my wrist and elbow I felt a sharp nail piercing my skin from the inside. I knew it was a piece of my bone. Then everything went black around me.

When I woke up the next day I was home in my bed with my mom sitting beside me. She kissed me on the cheek, and told me I had spent the night in the hospital.

I stayed home from school for two days and ate chocolate mousse, croissants, and onion soup that Aurora delivered. Buddy visited me once. He had some black and blue on his cheek where Rayjohn landed his punch, but otherwise, he was fine. We talked about ways to get even with Rayjohn who didn't get any punishment for breaking my arm. He said it was an accident.

"I didn't know his arm was under my foot," he said. *What a lie!*

"We need to get him away from his gang," said Buddy. "He won't have so much power then."

"And how do we do that, Buddy? If you went to my school you would find out that everyone in the school is afraid of him, even the teachers. Nobody does anything.

When there's a playground fight, the kids take bets on how long it would take for the poor kid to be down on the ground begging for his life. It doesn't take long. I've already watched three fights, and it's only the end of September."

"Do you bet too, Davy?" He looked at me in a way that made me feel guilty.

"No, but I watch, and I don't do anything, and I stand way in the back of the crowd. I can't be a snitch. I'd be the next little kid screaming for my life.

And I'm no match for Rayjohn in a fight." I held up my left arm wrapped in a cast. "Maybe if I were a six foot one inch quarterback like you I would have the guts to go after him."

Buddy put his hand on my shoulder. "And I didn't save you from him that night. In fact, you were trying to save me. You've got the guts, little guy. And for your information, Rayjohn is the coward."

The phone rang. It was Aurora.

"You broke your arm? Are you bedridden? No, well then I expect you here at 9 o'clock sharp on Saturday. What arm did you break?"

It had been two weeks since Rayjohn broke my arm, and I hadn't been to work at Aurora's. Wearing a cast was no fun. But I was back at school and feeling ok.

"The left one," I said.

Then you can work with your right one. You are right handed, aren't you?"

"Yes, but I am still a little weak."

"I understand," she said. "You will be working in the library stacking books. But you can take as many breaks as you need."

A SPIDER IN THE LIBRARY

SATURDAY MORNING I walked up Watson drive toward her house. I was feeling pretty good. Mom gave me some aspirin for the pain in my arm, which was not too bad now. I liked the smell of autumn, sweet and earthy, and the sound of crisp leaves crunching under my sneakers. I was hoping I could work outdoors. Stacking books sounded like a boring indoor thing.

My life had changed so much since last year. I once lived in a big house, a new house, with a basketball hoop in the driveway and a swimming pool in the backyard. I could picture the pool closed for the fall, the canvas covering filling up in the center with rotting leaves. I had a happy mom then who baked cookies and bread and who went to my games and cheered for my team, who played Garth Brooks CD's and danced by herself in the living room. DIVORCE, the ugliest word in the universe.

I walked up the incline of the driveway, a semi circle. A limo could drive up and let passengers off right at the front steps of the mansion. I pressed a round button on the side of the door. I jumped back when a deep sound echoed from inside.

Aurora came to the door in her chef's outfit, smiling.

"Ah, David, right on time." She looked at my cast which went up my arm from the wrist to just below my shoulder. "I see you have some signatures and drawings. You must have a lot of friends. I'd like to write on it later."

I didn't think I had a lot of friends. It's just when people see you with a cast they all want to sign it, just because. Some names and some smiley faces were written on it. The girls like to do little flowers. One even wrote Her phone number. Embarrassing! No one paid attention to me before Rayjohn broke my arm. Guess he did me a big favor!

"Your work today should not be too hard. But it is very important to me.There is a library on the second floor. My dear Louis did his work there. The shelves are empty. His precious books are in boxes. I would like you to put the books on the shelves alphabetically by the author's last name. His name was Louis Gardner. You will see his name on a few of those books."

I followed her up the spiral staircase that ended in a hallway. I could smell books, like at the library in town. Books have an odor, almost the same as a church odor, though I'd only been in church twice, for a funeral and a wedding, a long time ago.

She turned the knob of the first doorway on the right, and led me into a large room. Wooden bookcases, mostly empty, lined two walls floor to ceiling. Light streamed in through a round stained glass window facing us. Ribbons of light, blue, orange and yellow covered everything in the room. A large roll top desk took up another wall. A swivel chair waited for a man to sit down at the desk and get to work. Above the desk the antlered head of an unfortunate buck looked at us with glowing glass eyes.

Three cardboard boxes filled with books sat in the middle of the room next to a ladder. Aurora pointed to them. "Alphabetical by authors last name, David. Sort first, then shelve starting with the top left shelf."

She looked me in the eyes. "Are you ready for this?"

I nodded, but I wasn't sure. "Well, do as much as you can. You don't have to finish it today, and take some time to read something that interests you if you need to rest. I'll be downstairs cooking. If you need me just pull the cord hanging by the door. The bell will ring in the kitchen. Oh, and I don't mind if you sit in Louis' chair and just read. This is a fine room for that, don't you think?"

"Yes, ma'am." I heard her steps get softer as she went down the staircase. Soon piano music made its way up stairs. The kind they call classical, I think. It was good to listen to while I got to work.

So many old books! I took her suggestion and made piles according to the alphabet and the authors' last names. Louis Gardner must have been a smart man if he read all these books.

I found ten books that he wrote and put them in the "G" pile. Five of the books were about God and Jesus. At least their names were in the titles.

One book was big, flat and thin. It would stick out on the shelf, so I put it on the side of the pile. Louis Gardner stared at me from the back cover. He had dark hair and dark eyes and a mustache that turned up at the ends like a hairy smile. I would have liked him.

I had twelve books in the " A " pile so I carried two or three at a time up the ladder and started filling the top shelf. When the "A" books were done, I was tired and both my arms were sore.

Ok, she said I could read and rest. I picked up Louis' book

and sat down in his swivel chair. "I hope you don't mind, Mr. Gardner."

I rolled the chair closer to the desk, put my feet up on the desk top, and settled in. I thought that Mr. Gardner winked at me from the back cover. It had probably been a long time since someone read his book.

The front cover was glossy like a photograph. It was the spider motorcycle, all spiffy shiny black against a cloudless blue sky.

THE SPIDER CYCLE: BIOLOGY AND TECHNOLOGY HIT THE ROAD TOGETHER.

The book was mostly photos and diagrams of the various parts of the cycle and how they come together. But there was a whole section about spiders, the live kind. Colorful photos grabbed my attention.

Science is my favorite subject. I usually get A's or B pluses depending on the teacher. This year I was lucky to get a C. Mom and Dad were too busy with the big D to even notice.

A diagram showed the heart of the spider in the center part of its body. According to the arrows, spider blood is pumped by the heart through the whole spider. It is the pressure of the blood going through the spider's legs that gets them to move. The more pressure, the faster they go. A spider has eight legs, so it can go pretty fast.

I wondered what that had to do with the big black spider motorcycle. I thought there must be a gas tank in that thing.

Maybe there's a blood tank. Maybe Aurora needs blood fuel for the spider cycle. Maybe she needs human blood. My blood?

I needed to do more research.

15
CHAPTER

A SLICE OF KEE'SH

I HEARD THE bell ring for lunch. I wasn't done with the books, and I hoped that wouldn't matter. I put Mr. Gardner's book on top of the desk.

The smell of baking bread reached my nose as I walked down the stairs. But there was an added aroma this time, bacon, unmistakeable. I love bacon!

I made a stop at the restroom, then entered the dining room. Two blue plates were set across from each other on a red and white checked cloth. She had filled a large orange and blue ceramic bowl with red apples, purple grapes, and yellow bananas. I sat in the same chair, and Aurora poured water into the glass. I drank it right away. She refilled my glass . A repeat of last time, it seemed.

"The pie is ready. I must get it from the oven before it burns." She put the water pitcher on the table and headed into the kitchen.

She came out with a large pizza tray.

A good old pizza.

"This is not pizza, David. It is quiche (kee' sh). Big difference."

Does she read minds, too?

She set the tray on the table and cut into the bacon smelling pie.

I knew I was going to like this. She placed a large slice on my plate.

I lifted my fork.

"No, no, David! Remember what we must do first!"

I put down the fork, bowed my head and put the palms of my hands together like Aurora.

"Father God," she said, "thank you for the chance to cook for David again. The work he is doing in Louis' library is so important. I hope he has looked at some of the books. We pray that you heal David's arm and bring him back next week to help me. And keep him safe from the bullies, Amen."

"Amen," I said.

"Dig in!" And I did. The crust was crisp and buttery, the filling, a light creamy mixture of scrambled eggs, bacon, and some bit of veggies. It probably had some secret French ingredients, too. "Magnifique!"

"Have as much as you like. I have two more quiches in the oven, and you can take one home to Linda and Kelley.

David, I'm sure you noticed a lot of books about God. My Louis was a minister. He read all those books and even wrote some. Do you know about God?"

I had a mouthful of quiche so I shook my head, "No."

"Ah, so many things to teach you! While you're eating I will tell you a story about another David." She put a large book with an old leather cover on the table. On the book's spine in gold capital letters was the word HOLY BIBLE. I had heard about this book.

"David was an important person in the Bible. He was an

ordinary boy, like you, who became a great king. Do you ever think you will be a king, or President of the USA? This David didn't either. Of course, there was no USA then."

I was ready for another piece of quiche and more of the crusty bread in a basket beside me. I was happy to let her speak so I could eat.

"David was the youngest of eight boys. His father's name was Jesse. They lived in Bethlehem, a place you might know. You hear of Bethlehem a lot around Christmas. They were all nice boys, big boys, except for David who was small. They all worked on Jesse's farm, even David who watched the sheep."

"Like he was a babysitter for sheep, or something?" It sounded like that could be fun.

"Yes. He was a shepherd. But it wasn't easy work. He had to keep the sheep safe. Lions and other creatures were always trying to attack the sheep. He didn't have a gun, but he made himself a sling shot and practiced with it often. He knew where to aim to kill a lion or bear with just a rock."

"That's cool," I swallowed a mouthful of pie crust. "I could use a sling shot to fight some bullies at school."

"David was so good with a sling shot that he saved his people by killing a ten foot tall giant named Goliath. He became a hero after that, even though he wasn't very big."

"Is that a true story?"

She held up the Bible and shouted, getting me to jump out of my seat. "Everything in this book is true!"

Aurora put the Bible down beside my plate and began clearing the table as I worked on my third slice of quiche. I picked up the Bible and looked through it for the story of David. I couldn't find it. There were too many pages, too many strange words.

She came out of the kitchen with two small plates and placed one in front of me. An oblong tube of crust under a blanket of whipped cream sat on the plate.

"Eclairs for dessert. Dig in. There is a surprise inside."

I sunk my fork into the crust and vanilla pudding oozed out of the tube. I tasted it. More yummy than the mousse last week! I hoped she packed some for me to take home.

"I love to cook for people," she said as she handed me a large sack I knew was filled with delicious leftovers.

"Thank you, ma'am. My family will love this."

"Oh, if you want to know more about David I have a small Bible for you. My husband had many of these to give to children."

Children? I no longer put myself in that group. I was in 8th *grade, a Senior in Middle School!*

When I finished the eclair she put another on my plate. I couldn't refuse.

She is trying to fatten me up for some reason. Hansel and Gretel is just a fairy tale. Aurora seems too nice.

"You have gained some weight since I've been feeding you." She smiled proudly.

Did she read my mind?

"You were far too thin. You needed some meat on your bones to handle those bullies. And if you want to know how the Bible David handled his bullies, because he had many, read about it!"

She put the small Bible into the bag with the food, and handed me three more ten dollar bills, and a five.

"Oh, let me sign your cast!" I waited while she found a Sharpie in the kitchen. She chose a spot on the underside of my wrist and wrote something. I didn't see what she wrote.

16

CHAPTER

WHO IS THIS OTHER DAVID?

I WALKED DOWN the four steps to the circular driveway and turned right just to get a glimpse of the shed. It was mostly hidden by tall weeds and tree branches, but there seemed to be a sliver of light coming out from the window. Maybe there was a hole in the curtain. There is a reason why Aurora told me not to go near the shed. Sooner or later I was going to find out.

School was getting better although I was still on my guard for the Mafia. I knew Rayjohn was out to get me. But since he broke my arm a lot of kids were friendly. They wanted to sign my cast, so I had to keep a marker in my back pack. I met another geeky kid who lived in a house two blocks from the apartments. So I didn't have to eat lunch alone, and I could walk most of the way home with my new friend, Josh.

I put Aurora's children's Bible on my nightstand. I took a flashlight to bed with me so I could read late into the night. At first I thought the Bible would be hard for me to read. But it wasn't. Maybe the children's version was a good starter for me.

Aurora put book marks on the parts that were about David. Finding out about him was like putting together pieces of a puzzle. There was a young David, a teenage David, a King David, and an old King David.

It all started with a bunch of people, way long ago, thousands of years before year one, the year when Jesus was born. The time of David was BC (Before Christ). I thought Jesus must be so important that we count all our years starting from his birth. "Plus time" started with him. Before Jesus was born was "minus time." David lived around 1,000 BC (Before Christ) counting backward from year one.

Anyway, there were these people, the Jews. God loved them. He looked out for them and wanted them to be the best people on earth. That's why he gave them the Ten Commandments, so they would know how to be good folks. They would be the role models for the rest of the people who did very bad things. The Jewish people had many enemies among these bad people.

The Jews thought they could do better fighting enemies if they had a king to lead them. So they asked God for a King. God asked a wise man called Samuel to find them a king. Samuel found a man named Saul who seemed like he would be a good man for the job. God said Saul would be fine. So Samuel made him King of Israel by pouring oil on his head. That's called anointing.

God also talked to Saul when he became king. He told Saul what to do and expected Saul to obey him. Saul's army defeated many enemies of the Jews. But after a while, Saul stopped following God's orders and did things his own way. God got angry with Saul and told Samuel to find another king.

A man named Jesse lived on a farm in Bethlehem. God told

Samuel that one of Jesse's sons would be a great king. Samuel met Jesse's seven older sons, but God did not choose any of them.

"Do you have any other sons?" Samuel asked Jesse.

"Yes, there is David, but he is young and small. He is out in the field taking care of the sheep."

Samuel found David in the field, and God said, "Yes, David is THE ONE!"

I can't imagine what David thought when Samuel told him that God wanted him to be King of Israel. Samuel took out the can of oil that he carried around just in case God asked him to anoint someone king. He poured it on David's head and said some prayers.

David was anointed, but he wouldn't become King of the Jews for about seven years. If I were him I'd just like to take a shower and get the oil out of my hair. I'd just like to get back to my sheep, or kill some lions with my slingshot.

David also liked to sing and write songs. He played a lyre, a stringed instrument like a small harp or guitar. He was very talented. Maybe that's why God chose him to be the second King of Israel.

Anyway, that's as far as I got in the Bible. I didn't see that David and I have much in common except for our names, and being small for our age.

I knew God wouldn't pick me to be special. I didn't even know God. My family doesn't believe in him.

17

CHAPTER

D IS FOR DAVID

THE MAFIA WAS leaving me alone, but I sensed them circling me at a distance. At least now I was getting to eat my lunch. Mom was packing bologna sandwiches, pickles, fruit, and eclairs. Oh yes, I gained 5 pounds and almost two inches since school started, finally hitting the growth spurt!

The Mafia had taken over the basketball court, so I couldn't practice anymore. They had another member, a really big guy, taller than Rayjohn. They said he had a wingspan like LeBron James. His name was Barticus Maximus.

The high school team still needed to use the court for practice and some scheduled games. Rayjohn and the Mafia would not permit it. This was a real problem. Buddy tried to talk to Rayjohn, but he wouldn't budge. The high school team was mad, but not mad enough for an all out battle for the basketball court. At least not yet!

My arm was healing. The cast with all the writing and pictures was off, and I put it away in my closet. Now, I could stack books using both hands which was good for building muscle, according to Aurora. But since the weather was still warm, she had me working out doors.

Lunches with Aurora were longer and bigger. Last Saturday it was beef bourguignon, a beef stew with wine. Aurora said it was ok to eat the gravy because the alcohol evaporated in the cooking. She put vegetables in the stew for color and vitamins. I brought home lots of food for mom and some recipes Aurora copied onto note cards. So I was eating good at home too.

Aurora asked me what I had learned about David, the Bible guy. While I was digging into the beef stew she told me more about him. The Jews were fighting some mean people called the Philistines. They were so bad that they sacrificed children to Baal, a made-up god they worshipped. The Jews worshipped the one true God. The whole Bible is all about that God, the good God, the one and only God.

David's older brothers went off to fight the Philistines. They had joined Saul's army but they wouldn't let David go with them.

One day David went to the battlefield to deliver some supplies to his brothers. He was too young and small to fight, but he wanted to be part of Saul's army, so he hung around to watch the battle.

The Philistines had a secret weapon, a 10-foot tall giant. The deal was that if the Jews sent one man to fight Goliath there was no need for a big bloody battle. If Goliath won, the Philistines could take the territory from the Jews. If Goliath lost (got killed) the Philistine Army would turn around and go home. But who could fight a 10-foot tall giant? No one volunteered.

"I'll do it, pick me," shouted David. He came out of the crowd of soldiers and stood in front of the Army of Israel. He was just a small boy! Maybe his voice cracked, like mine.

King Saul was even afraid to fight Goliath. When David came forward, he tried to discourage him, but David insisted. So Saul gave David some of his armor for protection. But he was too small for Saul's heavy metal vest, which would only get in the way. He said he didn't need it. He knew he had a secret weapon in the pocket of his tunic.

David faced Goliath across the battlefield. As he walked toward the giant, he bent down near a brook to pick up five small stones. Then he started to run toward his enemy. When he was close enough, he took out his slingshot and loaded it with a stone.

Goliath's large head was an easy target, an easier target than the lions he killed to protect his sheep. He circled the leather sling three times around his head, then released the stone with a flick of his wrist. In a second the rock hit its target. **One blow to his forehead and Goliath went down!**

So that is how David became a hero to the Jewish people. But it is only the beginning of his story.

18
CHAPTER

DAVID AND COREY PICK APPLES

AURORA HAD A large backyard scattered with old oak and maple trees. Three craggy apple trees heavy with ripe fruit stood at the far end. She handed me a bushel basket and told me to go fill it. I climbed a ladder leaning against the tallest tree. When I got to the last rung I heard a familiar voice.

"You need some help, Davy?" It was my little friend Corey from across the street.

"I'll toss you a basket and then I'll start throwing apples down. You can catch them and put them in the basket."

Corey jumped up and down and laughed. "OK, ready!"

The basket landed upside down on Corey's head. He quickly removed it and placed it beside him on the ground. It seemed funny, so I laughed. His face got angry.

"I don't play games, Davy." He quickly turned and started running across the lawn toward his house.

"Corey, I'm sorry I laughed at you. I hope you aren't hurt. Please stick around and help. I really like that you help me."

He stopped for a second, turned and ran back to his position by the basket. "Ok, Davy, pitch those apples to me."

He crouched down like a catcher on a baseball team. I used my best pitching skills, and together we filled the basket.

Standing high up on the ladder, I noticed a beam of light flash across the yard. The sky was darkening in that direction. Lightning? No thunder sounded. The light came again from the shed, from the window with the torn curtain.

"Look, Davy, a tiny house. I saw a light. We could have fun playing in it."

"Off limits, Corey. Don't go near it. Aurora's rules!" I tossed him a ripe apple. "Wipe it on your shirt, and enjoy!"

He smiled as he caught it, showing a mouthful of crooked teeth. I climbed down. We grabbed the handles of the basket on both sides and walked to the back steps with the basket between us.

Aurora rushed out the kitchen door to greet us. When she saw all the apples, she laughed like a little girl who got a new doll for Christmas.

"You must both take some home." She handed us plastic bags from Food Circus. "Here, choose some ripe ones. I will make some apple tarts with the rest."

"That will be a lot of work," I said.

"Ah, yes, but I have a plan," she winked at me.

"I hope that plan doesn't include me peeling apples."

"Wait and see, David."

Corey took his bag of apples, and I walked him across the front lawn to the street.

"Do you think these are poison apples, David, like Snow White ate?"

We both had already eaten one."Well, I'm not dead yet. Thanks for your help Corey. Adios Amigo. That means goodbye in French. I think that's French."

"No, it's Mexican. My mother's cleaning lady says that to us when she leaves the house."

"You sure?" I hated to be corrected by someone younger than me.

"She says,'amigos', which is plural, you know, for more than one friend. Hey I am six years old, but I'm in third grade. Do the math. That means I skipped two grades.

I was bored in kindergarten, so I did some fun things to keep my mind going. I sneaked into the classroom, erased the 1 plus 1 equals 2 on the board, and wrote 1 squared equals 1. The teacher called me a wise guy, not in a nice way. Can you believe the kids all thought that pi was a dessert? Do you even know what pi is? Hint, it has something to do with math!"

"3.14. Right!" I answered him. *I'm not so stupid.*

"Yes. It is a ratio of a circle's circumference to its diameter. So the teacher sent me to the principal, who sent me to a lady who gave me a long test with a lot of puzzles and questions, like who invented the light bulb. I knew it was Thomas Edison. Then, they put me in second grade and other special classes for really smart kids. But I'm still bored in school."

"Corey, when my mother wasn't smoking and drinking she would say things like 'Never judge a book by it's cover.' Stick with me amigo, I have a feeling that I can pick your brain. Oh, and if you are bored, get on the internet and find out about spiders, the creepy crawly kind." His brown eyes twinkled as he broke into a crooked tooth smile, turned, and ran across the street to his house.

As soon as Corey was inside his front door, I heard a loud crash of thunder and felt a few raindrops on my cheeks. I headed back to the house and saw Aurora standing on the porch with an umbrella and a large sack.

"This storm is going to last awhile. I packed lunch for us to take to your house. Would you like a ride home in the Spider?"

Sure I wanted a ride. But in a thunderstorm, in a sidecar, in a motor cycle that could be a real gigantic insect? Kelley wouldn't think twice.

"Yes, ma'am. I'll take a ride. Thank you."

She pressed a button on the wall, and the garage door opened. Voila! There it was, two front legs extended off a smooth leathery body. Tires, like round rubber boots, grew out of each leg. The thing crawled silently toward us.

The book I'd left on Louis Gardner's desk told all about the Spider. It moved because blood flowed into its legs. A heart pumped the blood at different speeds to cause movement. A spider this big would need a lot of blood. But who's blood?

A flash of lightning lit up the spider. Two hooded eyes on his scaly head opened and glared at me. Under them a thin mouth appeared to grin at me.

I want to suck your blood, Davy. I heard him say.

19

SPIDER RIDE

THE DARK THING creeped down the driveway and stopped next to Aurora. She pressed a button on a remote in her hand, and a seat, like a leather recliner, came out of the right side. She reached in a storage bin behind her seat, pulled out another black helmet, and handed it to me.

"David, please take this sack of food. Put it in the trunk and slam it shut. Put on this helmet, sit in the sidecar, and strap yourself in for the ride."

Another fiery streak cut through dark clouds. The surface of the Spider glistened in the flash of light. It had an oily slick feel, not like metal. I had never touched one, but I imagined that a snake would feel like that. I shivered.

I sat down in the seat beside Aurora. She pressed another button on the remote, and a clear shield came over our heads.

"Spider, code 5," she spoke into a leather ear on the dashboard. An engine revved up underneath me. It tickled. I laughed. I heard a muffled chuckle from the driver, "Get ready for the ride of your life!"

The steering wheel reminded me of a snake coiled in a solid circle. She touched it and the Spider turned left at the end of the driveway. From the right lane of the cul-de-sac it seemed to turn left of its own will into the right lane of Watson Drive. Two beams of light came out from the Spider's eyes. A blue SUV was ahead of us. Two kids looked at us from the rearview window. One waved and I waved back. I wondered if they were scared. I would be. Aurora and I were both wearing black helmets that covered most of our faces.

The Spider turned into the apartment complex. A basketball game was breaking up on the court. People headed for cover from the storm. But I doubt that many of them missed our grand entrance.

"Holy Moly," I heard someone yell. "The creepy spider's back, and there's someone in the side seat!" A large crowd followed us in spite of the rain. Aurora parked in front of my building, slipped out of her seat, and unloaded sacks from the trunk.

"It's the old Spider Lady,"another person shouted.

"And looky here, it's Spider Boy."

I took off the helmet and stared straight at Rayjohn. Towering behind him was the giant, Barticus Maximus.

"That's him, Barticus, the creepy kid I was telling you about, little Davy. Looks like he has a new friend, a little old lady who drives a motorcycle!"

I heard laughter from the crowd. Every muscle in my body tensed with anger. He called my friend an "old lady," a little OLD lady. I remembered what she taught me about anger. Without turning my eyes from him, I took ten slow deep breaths. Then standing tall, head held high, carrying a bag of apples and a helmet, I walked inside the apartment building. I had just earned $35.00 and had the coolest ride of my life so far.

"Hey, Davy, I owe you one, remember!" I heard him shout as I closed the door behind me.

20
CHAPTER

DAVID DREAMS

AURORA WAS UNPACKING the sack of food that she brought, and Mom was setting the table with cracked china plates and paper towels that served as napkins.

"Linda, I love what you've done with your hair. Very flattering. It draws attention to your pretty eyes." Mom's eyes brightened at Aurora's compliment.

The compliment also caused me to really look at my mom. She was wearing jeans and a white sweater. Silver earrings peeked out of her reddish brown hair that skimmed her shoulders. She had a sparkle that I had not seen for some time.

"Why, thank you! I appreciate you recommending Molly. She is a great hairdresser. We talk about our lives. She has been divorced." Mom turned to me. "Davy, Aurora's staying for lunch since it is still pouring outside. I'll let you know when it is ready." I watched her put the casserole in the oven.

"Thanks, Mom. I have some homework to do, a project for science on spiders."

"Spiders!" Aurora turned around to face me. She had a curious expression, a half smile.

"Spiders are interesting creatures. We can learn much by studying them,"she said. "Some scientists study nature and take what they learn from it to create other things."

"Yeah," I nodded. "The Wright brothers watched birds fly and invented the airplane."

"Yes! Science starts with observing things. I may know a little about spiders. My Louis was a scientist."

"I thought he was a minister." I had shelved all those books in his library on God and the Bible.

"He was a scientist first, a biologist. The more he studied plants and animals, the more he was curious about the creator of all life. He started to read the Bible to get to know God, and then went to a college to become a preacher of God's Word."

"Science led Louis to the Lord." She bowed her head. "And he is with Him now."

"Well, I am going to find out more about spiders," I said. I thought about the book on Louis' desk as I went to my room, turned on my lap top, and settled myself comfortably on the bed. I opened Wikipedia to an article about hydraulics in spiders, read one paragraph and fell asleep.

Darkness came over me. My hands were locked on the leathery wheel of the Spider, steering into the night sky. Lightning sparked to my left and right. Something was behind me. I wasn't sure. It sounded like an angry engine gaining speed and getting louder.

I pressed a pedal on the floor and the Spider took off at 100 mph. Then the engine in the thing behind me got even louder.

I was terrified, but also curious. I turned my head to the left and saw it coming up on me. It was a spider, bigger and darker than mine.

A shadowy figure sat high in the cockpit.

21
CHAPTER

MORE FOOD FOR THOUGHT

"DAVY, COME AND get it!" I was close, so close to finding out what was behind me in my dream. I knew it was evil, and I was scared. Mom's call to dinner saved me, I guess.

"Beef bourguignon, perfect for a rainy day." Aurora took a ladle and scooped out large chunks of meat and vegetables from a crockery bowl onto the plates.

"Aurora, you've been spoiling us with this amazing food." Mom was seated, buttering a hefty slice of bread.

"Merci! But first we must thank the source, the one who brings us our food."

I knew where she was going, and I held my breath.

"Linda, at my house we say grace before meals. I would like your permission to do this before we eat. You do not have to say anything, or you can join me." Aurora looked at me out of the corner of her eye.

"Mom, I will say grace with Aurora." I bowed my head.

"We do not pray in my house. We are not religious. But I believe in God, even though he hasn't been good to us lately. Go ahead. I'll listen." Mom dutifully lowered her head.

Aurora filled the silence. "Dear Lord, thank you for bringing us together and for this meal which you have provided. Please bless David and his family and this food to nourish us all. In Jesus' name we pray. Amen."

I looked at Mom. Her lips were tight, but her eyes were soft in the afternoon light. "Amen." She whispered. I reached out and took her hand. A quiet energy flowed around all of us.

"Well, dig in!" We needed no second invitation from Aurora. While we ate, she spoke.

"I was born in a small town near Paris in 1932. My father was a doctor, and my mother was a Jewish woman who loved to cook. You know history, David, right?" She looked at me, and I nodded my head. I knew that France is a country in Europe.

"France and Germany were enemies then. Germany was ruled by a very bad man named Adolph Hitler. Have you heard of him, David?"

"Yeah, the Nazis. They were bad guys. Hitler was like a head Nazi, or something."

"Yes," said Aurora. "My good life in France was over when Hitler's Nazis invaded France in the Spring of 1940. I was eight years old.

I lived in a pretty little town on the River Seine. I used to play on the shore, wading in the water, making sand castles on the slice of beach in front of our house. I remember the house was made of stone. On the day we left, the red rose bush by my window had its first bloom.

My mother packed four suitcases, one for each of us: mother, father, my little brother Henri, and myself. I held the handle of my small suitcase. It was not heavy. We got into a taxi waiting for us.

'Don't turn back, but don't forget,' my father said as the taxi moved away from the curb. 'We have to leave your childhood now,' and we had to leave our cat, Regine. I cried, but I did not look back.

We got on a train with other families and a crowd of young men in uniform. After many days and nights we came to a big city by the sea. We went from the train to a very large ship. We were at sea a long time, and I was sick, I remember. We were in a small cabin with another family. 'We're packed like sardines,' my mother said."

"Your family got out of France in time. You were lucky," said Mom. "Two of my father's relatives were killed in Nazi camps." Mom turned to me, "Part of our family is Jewish, David."

This was new information. "You mean Jewish like my friend Jonathan who celebrates Hanukkah when we celebrate Christmas? He gets a present eight days in a row." *I liked that idea.*

"And that means you are like the David in the Bible," interrupted Aurora, "and like Jesus, himself."

"Well, I wouldn't go that far!" Mom's fork fell on her plate as she got up and began clearing dishes from the table.

Aurora pushed back her chair, stood up and picked up some silverware. I told her to sit, as I went to the sink to rinse the plates to go in the dishwasher.

"Aurora, the lunch was delicious as usual. Thank you for preparing it. I think that you have been feeding David more than food at your house."

Blush color crept up Aurora's neck and onto her face.

"Mom, we have eclairs for dessert." My voice did that thing of going from low to high like I was asking a question at the end.

"I'll put some coffee on the stove. I don't mean to be rude, but religion is a difficult subject to discuss over lunch with a child."

"And the subject of World War II is hardly a topic for children. I agree, Linda." Aurora wiped a tear from below the rim of her glasses.

"But," I said, "I am not a child, and I want to know about these things. And I want to know more about David, the Big King David, and what happened to him after he killed the giant with a sling shot. It is a great story, and Aurora says it is true."

"Well, if she says its true, it must be so! Here, have one of her fabulous desserts." Mom pushed a plate of cream puffs in front of my face. I chose a small one and stabbed it onto my plate with a fork.

"Mom, I'd like some coffee, too, with lots of creamer, since I'm still a child." I had just started drinking the leftover coffee in the mornings after Mom left for work. She is on the early shift at Food Circus. She's a cashier in training. I am proud of her.

The smell of coffee brought some comfort and peace back to the table.

"Linda, your son is an intelligent and curious boy, uh, young man. He has been very helpful to me. If you notice, I have given him a raise."

"Yes, he is very bright and responsible. Do you have children, Aurora?"

She smiled, "Oui, I have a daughter Angelique. She lives not far, in West Chester, and she looks out for me. She and her husband have given me four grandchildren. I do not see them as often as I'd like. They are older than David, and are busy with school and other important activities. As it should be."

"Kelley and I hardly ever see our grandparents. We send them cards and gifts at Christmas. They always remember my birthday and Christmas, and send me money."

"That is the way of the world, these days. Even back then. We had to leave my grandparents in France to deal with the Nazis. But it is comforting that they survived the war and even visited us in New York in 1948 when the war was over."

"These eclairs are so delicious, Aurora, better than the expensive ones in the bakery department at Food Circus. Where did you learn to cook?"

"From my mother. She always said that providing good food is a way to show love. And for a while I did all the baking and catering for my husband's church congregation. The minister's house had a large kitchen, like the one in my home now."

"Where was your husband's congregation?" Mom asked.

"In Manhattan, blocks away from the World Trade Center, which of course you know is no longer there."

"Oh my, you must have some sad memories. I hope you weren't there when 9/11 happened," said Mom.

"No, I was close by at home with Angelique, but Louis and David, went to the twin towers to help rescue people and __ I'm so sorry. I must go home."

She rose from the chair and walked across the room. She took the black helmet from the table in front of the couch and placed it over her head.

"David, next Saturday, please come. I will need help. I want to fix up the shed before __" Her voice trailed off again at the end of the sentence. *Before what?*

22
CHAPTER

DAVY TO THE RESCUE

IT WAS THE week of finals. The Mafia stayed clear of me. Even the bullies, jocks, and nerds had to study. And I didn't have time to think about basketball, spiders, or Rayjohn.

After a long time of getting bad grades, I was set on making A's and B's on this report card. I needed to show people I wasn't a dummy. What people? Mom already knows I'm smart; Kelley only cares about cheerleading and boys; Dad knows without a doubt that I am a failure. If I grow up and win a Nobel prize for curing cancer, he will still think I'm no good because I didn't play pro football.

"Irresponsible, careless," he yelled when I accidentally set off a fire alarm in the kitchen. I was cooking a recipe for fudge. I had a craving for chocolate and thought I could make it myself. The recipe on the bag of chocolate chips looked easy,

I still hear his voice in my head, and I still feel the fear and shame. He grabbed my arms and pulled me to my room, then flung me on the bed.

"Real boys don't cook! You're a sissy, David. Not the son I expected. I'm leaving that mess in the kitchen for you to clean up. Then come back to the room and don't show your face until it's time for school tomorrow! Kelley and I are going out for pizza."

I spent Thursday night at home alone in my room, propped up by pillows on my bed. My books and papers covered a purple bedspread, a Kelley hand-me-down I hated. While I worked algebraic equations, I stuffed Cheetos in my mouth and wiped my orange-coated hands on the bed spread. I had to ace algebra and pre-chemistry. Cheetos was my brain food for an all nighter!

Mom was now working the late shift at Food Circus so she wouldn't get home until nearly 11 o'clock. After the store closes she has to help clean up and stock shelves for the next day.

I was trying to memorize The Table of Elements. How amazing that all matter comes from just 118 elements. I was thinking about Louis Gardner's book about spiders and mechanics. Maybe I'll be a scientist someday.

I heard voices at the front door. It was early for Kelley or Mom to come home. The key turned, the door squeaked open and footsteps made their way across the living room to the kitchen.

"Mom won't be home until eleven. David is in his room studying and probably has his earbuds in. I'll get some Coca Cola and snacks. We can hang out and watch a movie on TV."

"Cool, I think Spiderman is on cable." The muffled voice sounded familiar and definitely belonged to a guy.

Mom would have a fit if she knew about this. I wondered if this dude was going to stay long? I looked at my clock. Mom was due home in an hour. Loud orchestra music signaled the start of the movie. I couldn't concentrate on my chemistry.

I heard Kelley's high pitched hyena laugh above the sound track. This guy must be a real comedian. I want to hear some of his jokes. I got up from my bed, went to my door, and slowly opened it. I walked ten paces down the hall in my bare feet and stopped at the entrance to the living room.

The room was dark except for the TV screen. I saw the backs of two heads close together on the sofa. The dude was trying to put his arm around Kelley's shoulder. She giggled and moved away from him. Then he moved even closer to her.

I backed out of sight before I shouted, "Hey Kelley, just so you know, Mom's coming home in about fifteen minutes!"

"OK Princess, I'll go now." A tall husky guy stood up and walked to the door. Without turning around he raised his arm, waved and said, "Next time, baby, when we're alone." The door slammed. A minute later I heard a soft knock on my door. "Come in, Kelley."

She was wearing her cheerleading outfit. Her hair was mussed, and bright pink lipstick smeared outside the boundaries of her lips.

She wanted to thank me for saving her from whoever he was, and I hoped it wasn't, nahh, no way.! She has better sense and taste that.

"David, don't say a word to Mom. If you say anything to her I swear I'll find a way to make your life miserable!"

"Well. Thank you very much, brother, for saving me from, whatever." I imitated her voice. "It looked like you needed help. Who was that guy anyway?"

"None of your business, dear brother, and I could have handled it myself."

We heard the key turn in the lock. The front door opened and Mom switched on the living room light. She looked very tired.

"How often can you say 'paper or plastic' without getting tongue tied? I must have bagged a billion pounds of groceries. I'm going to bed. You'd better get to bed, too. Exams tomorrow! Study hard!"

I turned to Kelley and smiled, "Good night, Kelley, sleep tight."

"Yeah, right," she shrugged.

23
CHAPTER

SECOND CHANCES

I STUDIED CHEMISTRY until midnight, then drifted off to sleep. I must have put the pause button on the dream I had last week. It suddenly came back on right at the place it left off.

I was driving the Spider. It was night, no light except the blood red headlights of the Spider. I must have had my foot on the gas pedal, ah blood pedal. I was speeding down a road so fast that I felt a force pushing me flat against the seat. I saw headlights in the rear view mirror, flashing an eerie green light. It passed the Spider's left leg. It was another spider motorcycle,

Someone was in the open cockpit, a tall person, a faceless man in a black helmet. He came up on me, his deep voice echoed through the mouth piece, Darth Vader, himself. "You're a mess, David. You'll never be a man!" The vehicle passed me leaving a wake of bad smelling smoke.

The next morning I failed the chemistry exam. Question after question, I drew blanks except for the most obvious such as H_2O being the formula for water. One by one I saw my classmates hand in their papers and leave the room. I broke into a cold sweat.

Mr. Schneider put his hand on my shoulder. "Davy, you're having a rough time. Looks like you are dealing with a lot of stress. Your grades have improved a great deal from the beginning of the year. And your paper on hydraulics in spiders was A + quality. Take a break. Go home, get some rest, and don't worry. I believe in second chances."

Second chances! When I got home I made myself a bologna sandwich and washed it down with a glass of milk. I could have used some sleep after last night, but my body and mind were wound tight, tangled up in each other. I needed basketball.

I picked a warm hoodie and grabbed my basketball from the hall closet. When I ran down the steps of the building, a cold blast of wind hit me, so I zipped the hoodie up past my Adam's apple. Dead leaves swirled around my ankles as I dribbled the ball to the empty basketball court.

"Thank you, God. No Mafia in sight."

I stood at the free throw line and shot one that just missed the hoop. The ball bounced on the pavement. I got it and attempted a jump shot from the right. No point. I turned and dribbled the ball down the court to try for a three point shot at the other goal. Success! Feeling more energy, I drove the ball across court, scored another, and went to the free throw line to try again.

I stood at the line, concentrating, pretending that my team depended on me nailing the shot. I aimed the ball, secure in both hands, certain it would go exactly where I wanted it to go. "Whoosh!"

A ball came over my head from behind me in a perfect arc, like a kamikaze, right on the mark. It made a clean entry into the hoop. It bounced twice at my feet and rolled to the side.

A dark shadow came over me and bent over the basketball that came out of nowhere. I started to tremble. *Could this day get any worse?*

I turned around to face my fear, as I thought my Bible David would do, and there was a Goliath.

"Hey, David, I been watching you. You got some good moves."

It was not Rayjohn. It was worse. It was Barticus Maximus, Rayjohn's new best friend.

"If you want we could practice together for a while. I don't have to get home until 5 o'clock. Dad's cooking up sketti and meatballs."

The tone of his voice did not match his look. A wide open face grinned down at me through a fringe of black hair escaping from a baseball cap turned backward. There was a shadow of a mustache along his upper lip, and his chubby cheeks had some zits, like I was getting on my forehead.

So we took turns at the free throw line. He never missed. When you're so close to the basket it would be hard for you not to nail every shot.

I made one out of three shots.

"Don't feel bad. It's pretty easy for me cause I'm so big." He noticed I was embarrassed when I missed a shot.

"Yeah, I wish I were bigger. I could maybe get a basketball scholarship to some college." As I spoke, I missed another shot from the foul line. Barticus caught the ball and tossed it back to me.

"Here, David, just concentrate. Close your eyes and imagine the ball going in the hoop, nice and easy, then make the shot."

Sure enough, in slow motion, the ball went clean into the hoop.

"That's a tip I got from my dad. He played a semester in college. Then, he had to quit when I came along."

"I bet you could get a scholarship to any college with a basketball team."

He shrugged his wide shoulders and frowned. "Nah, I ain't got it up here." He pointed to his head. " I'm special, in case you haven't noticed. Special Ed, I mean. Can't hardly read. Numbers get jumbled up in my head. But I can sure play basketball. And I sometimes scare people because I'm so big, but I don't mean to."

"I'm pretty good in school. I could always do better, though. I failed the chemistry test this morning. I need to get A's so my father will like me." The last sentence slipped out of my mouth.

"Oh, we all want to please our daddies. My pops don't care that I don't get good grades in school. He says I have a big heart, and that's what counts. Hey, he's cookin up spaghetti and meatballs right now. Wanna come for supper?"

Mom was at work until 10 o'clock, and who knew where Kelley was hanging out? "Yeah, that'd be great, Barticus, if your dad won't mind."

"Nah, he'd like me to bring home a friend. He wasn't much happy with those other guys, especially the one with the big mouth who picks on you. I want to smash his face in, but I got to control my anger. I could do a lot of damage to him with this body!" We laughed as he pounded his fist on his chest. I pictured him lifting Rayjohn off the ground. He was begging for mercy. Then Barticus smashed him against the pavement.

"Call me Bart." I looked up at him and saw that his grin matched mine.

24

CHAPTER

SPAGHETTI ALA MAXIMUS

I GRABBED MY basketball and followed Bart out of the Hunger Height's gate. He turned right heading down hill on Watson Drive. I ran to keep up with him. But when he saw I was out of breath, he slowed down.

"Sorry, David, these legs sometimes go without connecting to my brain, if you know what I mean."

I thought about the Spider, and how blood propelled his eight legs. *Do spiders have brains? How do they know to go fast or slow?*

"So Bart, what's it like being in special education, if you don't mind my asking?"

"Just means I'm slow. They gave me all kinds of tests. They said I'm real smart, just that the wires in my head don't connect like other people's wires. Guys like Rayjohn make fun of me, too."

"I thought you were friends?"

"Nah. He latched onto me because I'm new here and I'm big.

Figured he could use me on his team. At first, I thought he was cool, like everyone seemed to know him, and then I saw that they were all playing up to him because they were afraid. So I did too for a while, well, I still do, Davy. But if he ever picks on you again, he won't know what hit him!"

"I was afraid of him, too, especially after he broke my arm. He's a bully. I stay away from him, but I hate that he takes over the school and the basketball court."

"Yeah, me too. Well, here's my house. Smell the spaghetti sauce? Yum! My dad makes the best in the world. The recipe comes straight from Italy." My mouth watered. Spaghetti was my favorite meal when Mom used to cook.

There were no trees in Bart's front yard, only parts of cars or trucks scattered on the dirt. A mangy dog barked and rushed at Bart from behind an old blue pickup truck parked in the driveway.

Bart bent down and picked up the creature, a black and gray little mound of hair caked with dirt, a dust mop dog. He held it up to his face and kissed it, and got a sloppy lick in return. "Meet my dog Sweety."

Sweety yelped at me when I reached out to pet her. Sweety was the size of my dog Doug's head. A sad feeling came over me. I didn't have enough money saved yet to pay the extra rent at the apartments to get Doug back to me.

Bart and his dad, Tony Maximus, lived in a small one story house filled with guy stuff. No "fru fru", nothing girly, just piles of old newspapers, Mechanics Illustrated magazines, an old upright piano, a sofa and two worn leather recliners side by side in front of the big screen TV. We had to go around stuff to get to the kitchen where Bart's dad was putting a fist full of thin pasta sticks into a pot of boiling water.

"Hey Pops, I brought my friend David home for dinner," he yelled. *I could never call my father 'Pops'.*

Tony Maximus was as tall as his son. He wore a white full-body cook's apron over coveralls. His short sleeved tee shirt showed off his football sized biceps, and the hairiest arms I'd ever seen. The apron was splattered in red sauce. He looked like he'd been caught in a machine gun massacre. It drew my attention to his beachball sized belly.

He reached out his hand and grabbed mine, pumping it with such gusto that I was afraid my arm would break again. My hand smelled of garlic for hours.

"I hope you like Italian, David. I made enough meatballs to feed the Army, Navy, and Marines."

"It smells good, sir. Thank you for having me over for dinner. Spaghetti is my favorite."

"Well, sit yourself down." He pointed to a small wooden kitchen table with two straight backed chairs across from each other. Bart came into the room with a folding chair and took a plate from a cabinet and a set of silverware from the drawer below it. The table was set with colorful chipped plates like Mom's, unmatched silverware, and paper towels serving as napkins. I felt right at home.

Spicy smelling steam floated above a large bowl of bright red sauce. Meatballs popped up to the surface. Next to it, Mr. Maximus put out a bowl full of thin spaghetti, wiggling and squirming to get on my plate. He handed me a serving fork.

"Go ahead, David, I can tell you are a hungry man. Top the carbs off with the sauce, an old family recipe. Don't be shy! We're all guys around here. Go on, take more meatballs, five or six, and garlic bread, fresh from the oven!"

After I'd filled my plate I noticed they both dug into the food, no ceremony, and no grace before the meal. I wanted to stop them, but that wouldn't have been polite, so I said a silent thank you to the Lord, both for the meal and for a new friend.

After dinner Mr. Maximus gave me a ride home in his pickup.

"So glad you came by, David. We do spaghetti every Friday night, then watch a movie. You are welcome to join us. In fact, please come by next Friday or any time! Bart needs a good friend since we're new here. We just opened a shop in town. We do repairs on cars, bikes, trucks, like this one here.

You wouldn't believe it but this here truck was a bunch of spare parts before Bart and I worked on it. He's got the brains of a mechanic, like me. Good brains to have if you need things fixed, and who doesn't need things fixed? The name of my shop on Main Street is MAXIMUS AND SON. If you need anything fixed, we're your men!"

I thanked Mr. Maximus for his hospitality and let myself into our apartment. Mom was still at work, and since it was Friday night I didn't expect that Kelley would be home yet. Aurora was expecting me at nine o'clock sharp tomorrow, so I went straight to bed.

25
CHAPTER

JUST MOM
AND ME

I SLEPT THROUGH the night with no disturbing dream. I woke up early and heard sobbing, no, wailing, coming from the kitchen. I bolted out of bed and into the kitchen where Mom was pacing back and forth, a cigarette in one hand, dripping ashes on the tile floor, and a crumpled piece of paper in the other hand.

"He's got her! I hate him! He stole my little girl. He has no right! I'll fix him! He can't get away with this! I'm her mom, and I may be poor but I have my rights! I'm a good mom. OK, I'm not the perfect little housewife, but I love my little girl!"

I went to her and gave her a hug.

"You'll never leave me, will you, Davy?" she said wiping tears from her cheeks with a kitchen towel.

"No, Mom. Is Kelley OK?"

"Yeah, I guess. She's with him ."

With him? With the guy we kicked out the night before?

"With who, Mom?"

"With her dad, your dad. He wants her." She shook the paper at me. "Here, read this!"

I straightened the wrinkled letter, and read:

Bingman and Buster, Attorneys at Law

2100 Main St.

This sounded too legal, too important, and too scary. Bible David would not hesitate to face bad news. *God, give me strength.* I read the document which was only a page.

"Comes the petitioner, Lloyd Arthur Kingston, seeking full custody of one Kelley Shelley Kingston, daughter, etc., etc."

That's all it took, just a page of words to tell me what I already knew.

"*HE DOESN'T WANT ME! HE DOESN'T LIKE ME! HE DOESN'T CARE!*"

Mom saw it differently. She thought she lost a daughter. I knew I lost a father. *I never had a father.*

"Mom, please calm down. You've been doing great. You got yourself together. You have a job. We have a nice place here. We both have friends.

We'll figure this out, Mom. We have each other. I have a job, too. And I have to go soon. You need some rest. Kelley will be OK at dad's. We'll get through this. We are not alone."

I made a pot of coffee and some toast, and we sat quietly for a while. I finally said, "He didn't want me, Mom. He wants Kelley." She reached out and covered my hand with hers.

"I'm sorry, David. Someday he will be very sorry for the way he treats you."

"And the way he treats you, Mom. Aurora is expecting me soon. You need some rest because you have to work tonight at Food Circus. I'm so proud of you!"

In that moment I knew what Aurora would do. "Mom, let's pray."

"Ha, I doubt that God would listen to us. I haven't been in a church for 20 years, and the few times in my life I prayed, things got worse. Except when we prayed with Aurora. It was peaceful and kinda nice. Do you think she's ok, now? Are you still afraid of her?"

"I trust Aurora, but she is still a mystery. Anyway, it can't hurt us to ask God for help." I folded my hands on the table in front of me and bowed my head.

"Dear Lord, we need you. Please be with us this day. We know we haven't thanked you in the past, and we haven't been good a lot. But we thank you now for all you have given us, especially for each other. Please keep Kelley safe."

I couldn't believe I said that.

26

CHAPTER

LOST AND FOUND

I WASN'T SURE what Aurora was going to ask me to do, indoors or outdoors, so I wore my puffer jacket and knit cap. It was early November and most leaves were off the trees and on the ground. Gusts of wind pushed against my chest. I fought my way up the hill. It would be a losing battle for control of the leaves, if she wanted me to rake them.

Kelley was on my mind. I hadn't heard from her, not that I'd expect her to call me on her cell. I had her number, but Mom kept the cell phone. And I wasn't sure what I would say to her. Sure, Dad would take good care of her, his golden girl. She could do anything she wanted at his house.

I looked across the street and saw a mangy creature, all skin and bone, near a garbage can that had been knocked over by the wind. It was picking through the trash.

What a poor, sad animal. A stray, a runaway? How can I just walk past? I should see if it has an ID, but I'm late already. Aurora doesn't like people to be late.

I picked up my pace. I thought it was the whining of the wind I heard. Then I felt something rub against my ankle forcing me to look down. I saw matted hair and an outline of ribs showing through reddish brown skin. It was shivering.

"Oh, you poor thing," I bent down for a closer look, and I knew.

"Doug, it's you. You found me." The metal tag I'd made with his name and our old phone number was attached to the faded red collar. My Doug was once big and heavy, too big for me to carry. I picked him up easily and held him like a baby. His long legs had lost much flesh and dangled limply from his body. But his dark chocolate eyes came alive when I looked into them and his tail wagged feebly.

"Thank you God. I love you Doug. Oh I wish I knew you were like this. I'd have done everything to get you to live with me."

I continued on my way to Aurora's knowing I was late and hoping she would understand the reason. If I didn't already have grounds to hate my dad, I had now. How could he let this happen to Doug, my Doug, our Doug?

She saw me coming up the driveway with the bundle in my arms, and came out to meet me. She did not look mad. She looked concerned.

"David, what have you brought me? Is this a dog? Where did it come from? It looks starved to death?"

I couldn't hold back my tears. She hesitated, then circled us in her arms.

"Bring it into the kitchen. I'll get it a bowl of water and see if it'll eat something. I was worried because you are late. Come in. Go right into the kitchen with it. The kitchen is the best place to put it. It can't mess up too much.

Sit down. I'll make some hot chocolate. Tell me why you are late and why you are crying so hard."

She got a plastic container from under the sink, filled it with water and placed it on the floor in front of Doug's face. He was lying by my foot. He looked up at me, then back at the bowl, and made no move to drink.

"It must be scared. Give it time."

"Please don't call him 'it'. He is not an 'it'. He is Doug, my best friend, my dog that I had to leave at my father's place when we moved. I found him on my way to your house. He was looking for food from a garbage can.

I didn't even recognize him. I walked right by. But he knew me, crossed the street and followed me. I almost stepped on him. Then I heard him cry. I bent down and looked into his face and he licked my cheek.

The tag on his collar had his name and my old phone number. I hate my dad. He let this happen to Doug."

She put a mug of hot chocolate in front of me.

"What a smart dog to have found you. We must try and get him to eat and drink. I have some pieces of leftover chicken and rice in the refrigerator. Those are easy for a starved dog to digest. He can stay here in the kitchen where it's warm and safe, for now at least."

She got a container from the refrigerator, found an old plate in the cabinet, cut up small pieces of chicken and added several spoonfuls of rice. She put it in the microwave for about half a minute. Then she placed the dish in front of Doug's nose. He sniffed it and looked up at me.

"Let him alone. I have a job for us today, right here in the kitchen." She pointed to the long counter next to the sink. Two large wood cutting boards and several small knives were ready for action. Around them were apples, fifty or so, plump and red. They're the same ones we picked a few weeks ago.

"Today you will learn a new skill. We are going to turn these apples into apple tarts. What is your dog's name again?"

"Doug," I said. "Can he stay here with me?"

"I suppose. I could not turn him loose in that condition, could I?"

"Thank you, Aurora."

She moved two stools beside the counter and gestured for me to sit and begin peeling the apples. As I grabbed one and started to butcher it with a paring knife, she said, "Stop! There is an art to preparing apples for baking. You must watch me first."

She held an apple in her hand, turned it around and admired it. Then she took a small instrument with the other hand. This appeared to be made for the task of removing the peel. She skimmed it over the surface of the apple making a long red ribbon.

"Now you try, David."

I took an apple from the pile. She handed me the instrument which I applied to the apple's surface. No ribbon appeared. The skin was like leather.

Aurora laughed, the cackling laugh that meant I was doing something wrong.

"You are holding the wrong end of the peeler. It is not hard. Don't give up. The apple doesn't bite and it doesn't bleed!"

27
CHAPTER

PEELING THE APPLE

AFTER A FEW tries, I was in the groove of peeling apples. I had skinned three when the sound of a gong echoed through the room.

"Someone is at the front door."

The gong sounded again.

"I'm coming!" She hurried out of the kitchen through the dining room to the large foyer. The old door groaned when she pulled it open.

"Is David here? He told me he needed some help."

"Corey, isn't it? Yes. We are peeling the apples you helped pick last week. Come in. We can use another skilled hand for this delicate job."

I forgot about Corey. He always came by to help when I was working outside. I had peeled five apples so far, and there were forty-five left on the counter. Peeling apples is slow dangerous work. The peeler has sharp edges, and is hard to control on the slick curvy surface of an apple. I had been peeling for fifteen minutes and had band aids on two fingers.

Aurora led Corey into the kitchen. He looked scared. He still didn't know what to make of her. Then Doug gave a weak bark, got up from his safe spot under the table, and went right to Corey. Corey did what every little kid does when a scroungy dog comes over to get some affection. He cried out, "Get away from me! I don't like dogs, especially ugly ones."

I figured Corey was afraid of dogs. I picked Doug up and held him. I noticed that the water bowl was nearly empty, a good sign. He just needed some love. As I cradled him in my arms, I explained to Corey what had happened.

When I thought Doug felt safe, I trained Corey to peel apples. Aurora prepared the pastry dough at the other end of the counter.

"I found out lots about spiders, like you asked me last week. I got on the computer and I kept going. It was great." Corey was excited to share what he had learned. I could see that Aurora was interested, too.

"OK, Corey, you're in the "gifted" program so I know you can peel and talk at the same time. What have you found out?"

Facts came out of Corey's mouth like a swarm of honey bees headed to the hive.

"1- Spider's weave silk. The silk is stronger than steel based on their weight.

2- They are arthropods with 8 legs."

"Ok, knew that,"I said.

"3-Their webs are actually strong strands of protein."

"Ok, makes sense," I said.

"I bet you never heard of Portia." He had that 'gotcha' look. "Portia is the world's smartest spider."

"So how can you tell if a spider is smart? Can you ask it who invented the light bulb? Can it solve an algebra equation?" I liked giving smarty pants Corey a hard time.

"Ha, ha, David. Portia spiders are smart because they learn from their mistakes!" Another gotcha look.

I heard Aurora's "Ah ha!!" When I looked in her direction she was kneading a large mound of dough.

"They are also the world's smallest spider. Brains have nothing to do with size, at least as far as spiders are concerned."

I thought about Rayjohn, "Yeah, I get that."

I knew Bart was smart, but lots of people thought he wasn't because he can't read real good. I bet that Bart learns from his mistakes, though.

"OK, that's all good information, Corey. What else did you learn?"

"You already knew that they move by hydraulics. Tiny hearts pump their own blood to their legs with different forces to get them to move at different speeds. And they can move real fast if you watch them. They know to move away from danger. That's where their smarts come in."

"Yeah, Corey, but do they have a brain like we have, that tells all the other parts what to do?"

I thought about the humongous spider parked in the garage. I could see its bright headlights staring at me, sizing me up.

Corey stopped peeling. He looked at the half naked apple in his hand and took a bite. He was thinking as he chewed. I hoped Aurora didn't notice.

"Well," he said after a big swallow, "I read that the Portias can make these huge webs, large for their size. And these webs are like brains. Like they can cover the area around the spider and send back messages about what's happening. The Portia decides what to do. Like the web collects the data."

"And the data is processed somewhere else in the spider. But where? The spider is so tiny."

I was suddenly hungry, not only for a bite of apple, but for more information.

"Gentlemen," Aurora had rolled the mound of dough into a thin sheet. "I see you have peeled many apples, enough for the next step. And I notice you have tested them for flavor. Do they pass the test?"

Both of us nodded, relieved that we weren't being scolded.

"And we shall see after a while if they carry any poison." She winked at us. "Now, take up your paring knives, and begin the slicing."

She took an apple, placed it on the wooden board, cut it in half as it lay on its side. She held up half the apple. At the center was a perfect star.

"You must first find the star in each apple. Then place the star face down and slice neat thin wedges all around. Just leave the core. Place the sliced apples in the large blue bowl. Do not rush. It is a simple task, but it must be done just right."

"Yes, ma'am," we both nodded with cheeks full of possibly poisonous apple.

Doug had fallen asleep. I took my jacket from the back of the chair, placed it under his head and kissed his matted forehead. Aurora kneeled down next to me and covered him with an old blanket.

"He will be fine, David, and yes, he can stay with me, provided you come by to walk him everyday."

I threw my arms around Aurora's neck and buried my head on her shoulder. 'Boys and men don't cry.' I heard my father's voice in my head. But I couldn't stop. She smelled of sweet butter; she smelled of vanilla; she smelled like a grandma; and I cried for a long time.

Corey and I peeled and cut at least fifty apples, then filled two large ceramic bowls with the pieces. Aurora poured sugar, cinnamon, and other secret French spices into the bowls, mixing them with the apples.

"The pastry dough is ready. The apples are ready. All I need to do is set the dough into the pastry pans, add the apples and plenty of butter, cover with pastry strips, and bake. Voila! You boys have done your job for today."

She took some money out of a drawer, counted out four ten dollar bills, and handed them to me.

"Ma'am, this is too much."

"Nonsense! You need to pay your helper," she nodded at Corey, "and you will need to get some dog food for Doug. Remember, you must be here tomorrow to walk him. I am an old lady and I cannot do that."

It was hard to leave Doug, but I knew he would be safe with Aurora. I gave Corey a ten dollar bill and thanked him for his help. Aurora walked me to the door while Corey stayed in the kitchen playing with Doug. "My mom won't let me have a dog. Just want to play for a minute."

On the walk home my mind was full of random information that led to many questions. Doug had been on his own for a while judging from his condition. *Why didn't I know?*

Portia spiders are small and smart. So what? What do I do with this knowledge? We peeled enough apples for fifty tarts. What is Aurora going to do with all those tarts?

A car sped past me. I heard my name above the engine pops.

"Davy, boy, did the old spider lady pay you, ha ha?" Rayjohn's ugly head popped out of the driver's side window of an old rusted red Mustang, "Got myself a new car. I could use some extra bucks! Ha Ha."

Was there a girl in the passenger seat? I thought I saw the back of a smaller head with a pony tail.

28
CHAPTER

GREAT MINDS

THE SPIDER CRAWLED into the garage as I walked up the driveway carrying a bag full of dog food and treats. Aurora stepped out of the cockpit dressed in her Sunday best, a pink and black tweed jacket over leather pants.

"I wish you would come with me to church next Sunday. It was a good sermon. The music, I don't understand too much. It is too loud. They call it rock, you know. The young people your age like it. I prefer the old hymns. But I am hungry, and I'm sure Doug is too. "Praise the Lord ! Let's have lunch!"

Doug was barking at the door between the garage and kitchen. He was all over me when I walked in the room, his tail wagging faster than a windshield wiper. He was beginning to look like his old self. He chewed on a bully bone while Aurora and I ate sandwiches of croissants, ham and cheese.

The kitchen still smelled of apples, cinnamon and butter. "Aurora, can I please have a piece of apple tart?" I couldn't believe

I didn't taste the tarts yesterday. We worked so hard to make them.

"Oh my, I should have saved one tart for tasting. Sorry, Davy."

She opened the freezer door where the tarts were wrapped in tinfoil and stacked from top to bottom. "Voila! We are going to make some money, David. We can all use money, can't we?" She smiled and winked.

I looked down at Doug curled up by my feet. Maybe this is a chance for me to make ten dollars a month for Doug's rent at the apartment. I hoped Aurora planned to share some of the profits from the sale.

"Are you thinking of a bake sale, ma'am?"

She grinned and chuckled. "Great minds think alike, but we will need a venue, a place. I can't open a store in my kitchen."

"We could sell them outside Food Circus where the Girl Scouts sell cookies every year."

"Do we look like Girl Scouts, David?" She giggled.

"Hey, I've got an idea, Aurora. The Saturday before Thanksgiving there's a football game on the big field by the apartments. Everybody at school has been talking about it. Rayjohn and Barticus are playing for Hunger Heights, and my friend, Buddy, is quarterbacking for the high school team. People will be selling crafts and food all around the field. We would fit right in! These tarts would be great for Thanksgiving. If we cut some up as free samples, I bet we could sell them easy."

She laughed and clapped her hands. "I knew there was a reason I found you! Excellent idea! We now have a plan! A project! A purpose!"

After Doug finished his lunch, I hooked a leash to his collar and took him for a walk around the cul-de-sac. He went ahead of me and set the pace. I loved watching his tail wag the way it used to before the Big D. I wished I could take him back home to Hunger Heights, but he was safer here.

I came everyday after school to walk him and play with him, and to make sure he was eating OK. Some days I found Doug tied to a tree with a long rope.

"It is healthy for a dog to spend time outdoors," she said. Once I even found the two of them together playing fetch with a tennis ball.

29
CHAPTER

THE SECRET IS OUT

AURORA BAKED THE tarts early in the morning of the game. We wrapped the cooled tarts in tinfoil and gently stacked them into boxes. We loaded the storage section of the Spider, and my mom came by with our old Chevy to take the rest of the tarts to the game.

Aurora handed me the extra helmet and I strapped myself in to the sidecar. She revved up the engine.I could feel the Spider's blood start to flow. The Spider hummed as we drove down the hill.

Mom had set up a long folding table with a few chairs along the sidelines at the forty-yard line. Corey had made a sign with a sketch of the Eiffel Tower and the words:

FREE SAMPLES OF GENUINE FRENCH APPLE TARTS
WHOLE TART JUST $9.99
PERFECT THANKSGIVING DESSERT

It was a nippy November morning. The bare tree branches lifted to the sun in an icy blue sky. "Football weather," as my father would say. Kelley was cheering for the high school team. Dad would be there to cheer for her. I felt a tightness in my chest.

We attracted a crowd as we drove through the broken gate that protected Hunger Heights Luxury Apartments. A crowd followed us as we parked near the forty-yard line.

"Tell us about your car, motorcycle, spider bike, whatever. Where can we get one? How much does it cost? What store or dealership?" Many people were curious. So was I.

Aurora was too busy to answer their questions. She was cutting up some tarts into small samples. She placed them on napkins around the table as quickly as hands reached out to grab them.

"Only one sample for each mouth, please. There is a young man at the end of the table. You pay him $9.99 and he will give you a tart and your change. Only one tart per customer, merci." She tapped a football player in the hand with a spatula when he tried to grab two samples.

The crowd lined up behind me. I took in a lot of ten and five dollar bills, some singles and change.

Then the players came out on the field and formed a circle around the two quarterbacks, Rayjohn and my Buddy. It was coin toss time.

The crowd moved back to their lawn chairs along the sidelines. Many people who had bought tarts stopped at the coffee vendors before settling in for the kick off.

We counted our earnings. Close to $200.00 and only twenty-five tarts left. We would probably sell out at half-time.

I heard heavy foot steps behind me as I counted the money. I looked up and felt relief as Tony Maximus' face beamed down at me.

"May I have a sample of these French tarts. I have to see if they are as good as my Italian ones."

I handed him one and watched him chew. His smile told me he approved.

"Delicioso!" He gave a chef's kiss putting his fingers to his mouth, making a loud kissing sound and pretending to toss it to Aurora.

"Merci, such a fine compliment!" She looked way up into Tony's face.

"You are as good a baker as you are a motorcycle driver. I am Anthony Maximus, at your service. **Maximus and Son Auto Mechanics and Fixers of Anything.**" He handed her a small card. She reached in her apron pocket and pulled out a similar sized card. "**Aurora Gardner, French Cook and Baker.**"

"Madam, if you need anything fixed I am at your service. Your tarts are buttery and Frenchy. You must try my Italian ones sometime. Can I look at your motorcycle? I like to see how things work. I have never seen a bike like this one. I have lots of questions."

"Oui, yes! Perhaps you can be of help sometime!"

The apple tarts were a hit. People were not saving them for Thanksgiving. I heard comments like "buttery smooth, melts in your mouth" and "better than what I had in Paris." The tarts were advertising themselves.

The home team looked fierce in red jerseys. Rayjohn, as quarterback, was a bad choice. But Barticus, the defensive end, was like a big red Mac truck. He could make up for a weak quarterback.

Buddy was quarterbacking for the high school team, who looked like winners in purple and gold uniforms. The Hunger Heights team won the toss and decided to receive in the second half. They would be on the defensive.

This gave Bart a great opportunity to show off his skills. The high school team could not score. Bart and his crew formed a fence around Buddy, my Buddy. I didn't want to be mad at Bart. I didn't know who to cheer for.

Tony Maximus and Aurora were having a good time inspecting the Spider.

"Sweet," he said as he rubbed his hand on the chassis. "So soft. It don't crack or break. Where's the gas tank?"

"Oh no, no gas," she shook her head causing the chef's hat to lean far to the right.

"What makes it go?"

"Spider blood?" I answered as Aurora shook her head again. I grabbed the chef's hat before it hit the ground. She gave me an angry look when I handed it to her.

"Just like my recipe for tarts. It is, or was, a secret."

"Sorry, but I read all about it in Louis Gardner's book," I said.

"I was hoping you would do some reading while you were in Louis' library. You may take the book and learn from it. I, myself, do not understand a lot of the mechanics. Perhaps your mechanical friend," she winked at Tony, "might explain things to you."

Tony bowed and smiled. "I would be honored, dear lady."

30

CHAPTER

GAME OVER

THE TEAMS FACED off at the fifty yard line with Hunger Heights receiving this time. Buddy grabbed the football and passed it to a wide receiver who carried it all the way to Hunger Heights' 30 yard line. Where was Barticus Maximus?

"Maximus is down at the forty yard line, bent over." The announcer's voice blasted over the field. "Is there a doctor in the house?"

Tony rushed from the sidelines followed by an athletic looking woman carrying what looked like a doctor's bag. Tony kneeled and put his hand on Bart's back. Bart's head was bent over close to the ground. Green liquid poured out of his mouth into the visor of his helmet.

"He's puking!" Tony shouted to the woman with the doctor's bag. Liquid with small white solid bits formed a puddle on the ground. He took the helmet from his son's head, then he took off his own shirt so he could wipe the vomit from Bart's face.

"Probably a touch of the flu. It's going around,"said the woman who introduced herself as Mary Riley, Nurse Practitioner, mother of one of the players on the Hunger Height's Team. "Get him home. He needs rest, lots of water, keep an eye on him. Not much you can do for flu but let it pass."

"Puke, yew!" Rayjohn crossed the field and stood over Bart. He started to gag. "Wipe him off, and get him back on the field NOW!" He barked at Tony Maximus.

"No way he's going back in the game. That's my son! He's sick and he ain't playing today."

"I'm his quarterback, mister, and I say he's going back in."

"And I'm a medical professional, and I say this boy goes home and to bed! You, too! Get away fast! The flu is very contagious."

The referee called, "TIME OUT" on his mike and came out to the field joining the small group around Barticus who was barely on his feet. He spoke to the lady and went back to his microphone.

Soon his voice blasted all over the field."GAME OVER! LEAVE THE AREA IMMEDIATELY!"

"Oh no, the Ref's puking too," someone shouted! Two cheerleaders were making a beeline for one of three outdoor toilets. Each had a line of people waiting and clutching their stomachs and turning pale.

People rushed to their cars or apartments. The referee was back on the mike. "We have a situation here, folks. This many people don't get sick all at once at a football game. This is not a flu thing folks. This is the result of food poisoning. The French tart is the cause. I ate one a while ago, and now, I gotta _" His voice trailed off.

An angry crowd formed around our table demanding money back. Tony Maximus did his best to keep order as Aurora, Corey, and I gave out all the money in our cash box. Aurora's face was red. She was holding back tears.

When we were finally alone she spoke. "There is no proof that my tarts caused this outbreak. My ingredients are always fresh and pure. I always use the same recipe and no one has gotten sick before."

I wasn't sick, but I didn't eat a piece of tart. Aurora was too busy to eat one. Mr. Maximus had a small sample piece and said he had a bit of a tummy ache. But Barticus had snuck five sample tarts before the game started.

"We coulda won that game easy. I'm sorry Davy. I know the quarterback is your best friend, but their defense was weak. I bet someone on the high school team poisoned the tarts, just sayin, probably not the quarterback. He looks like a nice guy, but who knows," Bart shrugged and clutched his stomach. "Still feeling sick. But I ain't gonna die from this."

Mr. Maximus frowned. "Don't go pointing fingers at anyone, Bart. Too early in the game to call the shots. My worry is for Ms Aurora. This whole thing was not her doin but right now she probably thinks it could be. This calls for an investigation."

"You mean the police?" I whispered so Aurora wouldn't hear.

"No, I mean you, me and whoever else was close to the kitchen."

"I gotta think about this. Maybe I'll bring a tart to Mr. Schneider, my chemistry teacher. He could find out what caused this, and if this has anything to do with the tarts."

"Good idea, Davy." Tony Maximus smiled. He turned and walked over to Aurora leaning against the Spider Mobile, wiping tears from her eyes with a napkin.

He kneeled down beside her and put his massive arm around her small shoulder. "Little lady, me and my son, and Davy, we got your back. Don't you worry your pretty head about this." A fluffy white cloud of hair rested on Tony's shoulder.

"God bless you, Mr. Tony." She sighed.

31
CHAPTER

OLD WOMAN SUSPECT IN FOOD POISONING

SHE WAS SITTING at the kitchen counter on a stool reading the latest edition of the <u>Derby Chronicle</u> out loud. Her face was still puffy from a weekend of crying.

"Aurora Gardner runs an illegal bakery in the kitchen of her mansion off Watson Drive. Many people in the community are upset with her. On Saturday she was selling her specialty, French Apple Tarts, to fans and players at the annual rivalry football game between the Hunger Heights Hustlers and the Derby High School Dragons. Many people ate the tarts during the first quarter and became sick. The police are investigating. No arrests have been made yet."

"I know you didn't sleep, Aurora, but have you eaten anything today?" I was glad I had stopped at McDonalds. I gave her the burger and fries I had left over. She took two bites and pushed it aside.

"I do not understand," she looked up at me and Corey. "My food is so healthy, but it caused so many to be sick."

"I have eaten a lot of your food, ma'am, and I have never gotten sick. I've grown two inches, gained fifteen pounds, and I'm a lot stronger. Nothing like a burger when you're sad, though. Try it with ketchup."

I took a small envelope from the bag. She cut a corner with her teeth, then squeezed the thick tomato syrup on the burger.

"At least there's some serving of vegetable," she laughed.

"Let me see. We are doing an investigation. Neither of you got sick on Saturday, correct?"

"Right," Corey and I both nodded.

She took a french fry and dipped it in ketchup. "At last something good." She swallowed and made a face. "This so called 'French Fry' is an embarrassment to the French."

"Bart and Tony both threw up. But they are ok now. Everyone at school who got sick was better today. They were talking about it all day. I took a tart to my chemistry teacher who said he could analyze the ingredients to see if there was any poison."

"That's good." Ketchup dripped down her chin. "I have no poison in my house that could cause such an awful thing. But you two?" Her eyes searched mine and then Corey's. "You did not get sick." She caught the ketchup in a napkin before it landed on her white blouse.

"I was too busy selling the tarts to eat any," I said.

"I didn't eat any either," Corey shook his head.

"Those who didn't get sick would be suspects, no? But we are innocent. Oui, yes."

"So where do we go with that?" I asked.

32
CHAPTER

MULCH BEFORE LUNCH

"APPLES, OF COURSE, apples! What about fairy tales like Snow White? A poison apple nearly done her in." Bart bit into a slice of pepperoni pizza. We were sitting at the table in Tony's kitchen on Friday night.

"But there is no Snow White in this story, except an old woman with snow white hair who is kind of mysterious. Mr. Schneider has no doubt that the poison was a small amount of pesticide sprayed on the apples, just enough to cause people to be sick for a little while."

"And to put the sweet lady in danger and ruin her reputation." Tony placed a plump chocolate cannoli on a plate in front of me. "Mange! Eat the Italian way."

"But we peeled apples all afternoon. Wouldn't the pesticide have been on the peels?" I bit into the cannoli which tasted like an Italian eclair.

"Mulch," said Tony, "surely the dear lady mulches. If she grows stuff, she mulches."

I had no idea. "What is mulch, Mr. Maximus? Aurora is too lady-like to mulch."

Tony's belly wiggled when he laughed. "Somewhere, in the garage or shed is a pile of mulch, garbage like egg shells, apple or potato peels, stuff that rots. It is good for the soil and for gardens. I myself mulch!"

"So I need to go to Aurora's mulch pile and find some apple peels and have Mr. Schneider put them under his microscope."

"Sounds like a plan, Davy," said Bart.

The next day, Saturday, Aurora put me to work in the kitchen. She was afraid her kitchen was not clean. Cleaning a kitchen is hard work. Now I understood more about my mom.

My father said the house was never clean enough. But my mom was always cleaning. When she wasn't cleaning she was cooking, doing laundry, shopping for food, making beds. She did a lot of stuff! And Kelley and I didn't help much. I never made my own bed or shopped for groceries until the big D changed our lives.

I wore rubber gloves to clean the oven. I had to reach far inside and scrub with steel wool. I sprayed awful smelling stuff all over the inside, then wiped it off with vinegar and water mixed. After an hour, the oven was sparkling. I stood back and admired my work.

I needed a break. Good time to look for mulch before lunch, ha ha. Maybe it's in the garage. It was a logical spot for a pile of mulch, and it was close by. I opened the door between the garage and kitchen and stood still. I was about to enter the dark home of the Spider who was sleeping peacefully. Would I wake him if I turned on the garage light? I found a flashlight in a kitchen drawer. It worked.

As I entered the garage, I turned the flashlight on and pointed the light to the back. After a few steps, I smelled something sour, maybe apples rotting in soil. I stayed close to the cement wall and focused the light on the ground until I came to the back of the garage. I stepped in something squishy like dog poop, but it smelled more like rotten vegetables.

Mulch! I got down on my knees and pointed the flashlight at the ground. I picked through mush finding nothing solid. Then further down, my flashlight beamed on a sliver of red. More apple peels popped out of the muck. I put some peel samples in a plastic bag, and turned back toward the kitchen door, forgetting to turn off the flashlight.

I heard a sound, a loud yawn. Red lights blinked on the Spider's body. One of the Spider's four hidden legs reached out toward me from its belly. I jumped over it, but it followed me. Just as I got to the first step in front of the door, I felt it twisting around my ankle. Then it pulled my leg so hard I thought it would come off at my knee. I fell to the ground on my stomach.

Before I could scream, the kitchen door opened. Aurora looked down at me and laughed that weird laugh. Nothing was funny to me. I thought my leg would come apart as the Spider pulled me to the front of the garage toward its mouth.

She had a remote in her hand and was pressing keys. "Lord, if you get me out of this I'll do anything you want for the rest of my life!" I cried out to Him as Bible David did in the Psalms.

God must have listened. The red lights went dim. The Spider's leg unwound from around my leg. I felt weak and shaky, so Aurora reached down and helped me up the stairs.

"You woke him up. He is grouchy when he wakes up."

I was trembling. "If you hadn't come, what would he have done to me?"

"Well," she smiled, "It is a good thing I happened to be in the kitchen and heard noises out here."

"Thank you for saving my life, I think."

And thank goodness I held on to the bag of apple peelings. Mission accomplished!

33
CHAPTER

BIRTHDAY SURPRISES

KELLEY'S BIRTHDAY WAS two weeks after Thanksgiving. I hadn't seen her since she went to live with my dad at the old house. I couldn't believe it, but I missed her.

Mom had taken up knitting again to help with stress and keep her mind off smoking. She made Kelley a scarf and hat from purple and gold yarn, her school colors. I bought Kelley a bottle of lavender-smelling spray perfume, her favorite.

Mom wrapped the hat and scarf in fancy pink paper, and tied the package with a gold ribbon. She put it in a Food Circus shopping bag. I wasn't so fancy. I just took off the price tag and dropped the bottle of spray perfume into the bag.

Her birthday fell on a Saturday, so I had to work at Aurora's in the morning. I planned to take the gifts to Kelley after I was done having lunch. It was a good three mile hike up the hill to our old place.

Aurora had me putting up Christmas decorations inside and outside the house. I put together a tall fake tree in the living room beside the piano. It stood eight feet high. Lucky the lights were already on it. I plugged the cord into the outlet on the nearest wall, and "Voila!" The spirit of Christmas welled up inside me.

Next, I took strings of outdoor lights to the front lawn. I started untangling them when Corey came over to help.

"She wants me to frame the doors and windows with these lights. There should be enough to put some strands on the pine tree. I can pay you, of course."

"Sure," he grinned. I noticed he had braces now like railroad tracks on his front teeth.

"Did you find out more about the poison tarts? My mom says that old woman is dangerous and that proves it! If you weren't paying me for this she would be mad that I was over here."

"Mr. Schneider said there was no poison on the apple peels, so maybe something was sprayed on the peeled apples."

Corey shook his head. "That doesn't make sense."

"No, it doesn't. Aurora doesn't have any pesticides or poison in the house. The police did an inspection."

He was wide-eyed. "How could any chemical get on the peeled apples?"

"Your guess is as good as mine, maybe better, since you're smarter than me. Everyone who got sick is OK now. No one is pressing charges. But a lot of folks have been mean to Aurora. She doesn't go out much anymore. She is sad that something she did could cause people to get sick."

Corey held the ladder as I strung lights along the front of the porch. It took until noon for me to finally plug the last string of lights into the outlet by the front door. Corey went home for lunch, and I had a grilled cheese sandwich and tomato soup with Aurora.

After lunch I crossed the cul-de-sac and rang Corey's door. A woman with a pinched face and curlers in her hair opened the door and glared at me.

It was just after 12 noon. Did I wake her up?

"You got some money for Corey? I'll take it." I handed her a ten dollar bill. She took it, scowled, and slammed the door in my face.

She must be in a bad mood.

I was not in a good mood myself, and I was tired from the morning's work. I had an uphill climb ahead of me.

The trees along the sidewalks of Watson Drive had lost all their leaves. The few evergreens in people's yards were not yet wearing their Christmas finery and stood on browned out lawns.

From a block away, my old house looked sadder than I imagined. My mom would be in the kitchen baking Christmas cookies about this time, if it weren't for the big D.

Boy, do we ever need a little Christmas! I got closer to my old house and heard loud music, heavy metal, not sweet Christmas carols. It rang sharp in my ears.

I saw cars parked along the curb on both sides of the street, and two were in the driveway. One was a beat up red Mustang.

Dad's car must be in the garage. I did not want to see him or the driver of the Mustang.

A musky sweet smell reached my nose. It was not Christmas cookies baking in the oven. It was the stuff called weed that Rayjohn tried to sell to kids. I looked in the front window and saw kids from the high school moving to the loud music. I was about to crash Kelley's sweet sixteen party!

I wanted to turn around and run home to my mom. But I had

to get those gifts to my sister. I rang the doorbell praying my dad wouldn't answer.

"Well, looky here." It was Rayjohn who glared down at me. "See what the cat dragged in, carrying a bag full of gifts. Santa's little elf; got something good to eat? I hope you got pretty pink cupcakes for your princess sister? Come right in, Davy."

He put his arm around my shoulder and pushed me through the door to my own living room. There must have been thirty people, upstairs and down: Kelley's friends, Rayjohn's buddies, some looking older like Rayjohn.

I didn't see Kelley at first. I was worried. He led me to the dining room. The table was filled with food, chips, dips and a large cake in the middle, not yet served. It was frosted in purple with gold and red butter cream flowers and writing that said HAPPY SWEET SIXTEEN KELLEY.

"Kelley," he shouted across the room, "my sweet princess! Looky who's here with gifts! Get over here and cut the first piece of cake for your little brother!"

She was in a corner of the living room talking to two girls from the cheering squad. They all held red plastic cups full of some drink. I could smell it. All of them were drinking the same thing, some right out of cans that said APPLE BEER.

Kelley wobbled toward us as Rayjohn handed me a red cup with smelly liquid inside. She didn't notice me, but came face to face with Rayjohn. He had a knife in his hand, a large knife from my mom's kitchen drawer. He pointed it at her, lightly touching her nose with the tip of the blade.

Was he teasing her? Before I could move to protect her, she grabbed the knife by the handle, pulling it out of his fist. With both hands she held it pointing the tip of the blade at the ceiling above her head.

Kelley brought the knife down and stabbed her cake, piercing the center of a large red rose. She cut out a big, jagged piece and scooped it up in her hand. Red jam filling oozed from her fingers to her cheerleading uniform. A lopsided smile lit up her face as she drew her arm back and hurled the gooey mess in Rayjohn's face. A fast pitch worthy of a major league pro.

The crowd laughed through the music, hard confused laughter. At who? Rayjohn or Kelley? He called her a name I can't repeat and lifted his fist to strike her.

I reached into the bag, pulled out the bottle of lavender perfume, and aimed the sprayer at Rayjohn. I got him in the eyes! I kept spraying until the liquid was gone. He stumbled around rubbing his eyes and cussing.

The silent crowd parted as I pulled Kelley to the front door. We ran to the wooded area at the back of my house. I hoped the crowd was shocked enough and good enough to delay Rayjohn and the Mafia and give us time to escape.

34
CHAPTER

ANOTHER SURPRISE PARTY

AURORA'S PLACE WAS three miles down hill. We could stay on the edge of the woods and hide behind trees. Rayjohn would probably take to the road in the Mustang, but the boys would follow us on foot. It's ok. His boys were not the brightest bulbs in the circuit. We could outsmart them if Kelley could get sober.

We cut through three backyards, and I was still pulling her along. She fell twice and skinned her knee, but after about a mile she got more energy. Good. We ran faster when we heard muffled voices behind us, the Mafia. They probably had some kind of weapon. Maybe the kitchen knife that Kelley dropped?

I wasn't sure about Rayjohn. I heard several cars drive down the hill. The party had broken up. We could hide out in the woods, but we could easily get lost, and it was starting to get dark.

"Davy, we have to stop. I'm gonna be sick."

"Too much Apple Beer, Kelley? Go ahead."

After she puked, she felt better, and we moved faster through the shadows. We had gone at least two miles, maybe more, then crunching leaves sounded about ten feet behind us. They were on our trail. We ran at full speed until it got too dark for us to see things in our path.

The moon came out from behind a cloud. The outline of a small building appeared ahead of us.

"Let's rest a minute," I whispered. We crawled through weeds until we came to a metal wall. The sound of sneakers on dried leaves passed by us on the other side of the building. On the street a car motor got louder, so I peeked around the wall. I saw headlights moving up a circular driveway leading to a large familiar house.

"Hey Mick," It was Jackson's voice. Two dark figures ran toward the head lights. " Mick, it's Rayjohn. Maybe he's got both of them in the Mustang."

"Kelley," I whispered, "we're behind the shed. We're at Aurora's. And she's inside the house alone with Doug."

The headlights went dark. Then we heard the doorbell ring, and Doug's loud barking. Then came banging, more banging, glass breaking, Aurora screaming, "Get out, get out, you hooligans!" Then no more barks or shouts.

"Does Rayjohn have a gun, Kelley?"

"It's possible. He's a scary dude."

"I wish you had your cell phone. We have to get to a phone to call the police. Corey lives across the street. We can run for it while they're inside. It's dark enough. There's bushes we can hide behind. Stay close and follow me, Kelley."

"Do you think he'll let us use their phone?"

"Sure. Corey's my buddy." Then I remembered his unfriendly mom.

We got to the steps of Corey's house. I told Kelley to hide behind a nearby bush. I climbed the three steps to the door and pressed the bell. A deep gong echoed inside. I waited. I tried again. Corey's mom opened the door.

I almost didn't recognize her. She was wearing high heels. Wavy blond hair fell to the shoulders of a fancy blue dress, and a gold necklace dangled from her neck. The scent of her perfume, familiar, like mom's, mixed with the smell of steak cooking on a patio grill.

"Can you help me, ma'am?" I stuttered. "I don't mean to bother you again, but I'm in danger. I need to call the police!"

Her hands were on her hips as she looked down at me. "You again! Now what sort of trouble did little Davy get into?"

The smell of charred beef got stronger as I heard a back door slam. A tall man carrying a platter of meat walked toward us.

"Suzanne, who are you talking to? Dinner's ready."

I knew that voice too well. I pushed the door all the way open and walked into the light. I shouted back out the door, "Kelley, come on in. There's another birthday surprise for you here."

"Well, well! Happy Sweet Sixteen, darling daughter!" My father was grinning from ear to ear at Kelley, not me. "Come join us. Suzanne, set an extra plate.

"No," he looked down at me, "make that two."

I was worried about Aurora and Doug. Obviously, I couldn't ask to use the phone and couldn't stay for dinner. Something was very fishy. I started to run out the door when Corey rushed down the stairs.

Corey shouted, "Rayjohn, Jackson and Mick just broke into the old lady's house. They're gonna tie her up and shut the ugly dog up, too. And then they're gonna take the Spider out for a ride!"

I was out the door in a second with no idea what I would do

next. Kelley was behind me. I saw that Mick and Jackson were moving the red Mustang that was blocking the garage door. We hid by the side of the garage and waited.

They parked the Mustang along the curb, clearing the driveway. The garage door squeaked open. We crouched down and entered, staying close to the wall and along the side of the Spider's body. I led the way to the back of the Spider, stopped and looked behind for Kelley.

No Kelley!

35
CHAPTER

CAUGHT IN
THE WEB

I HEARD HER scream. The Spider's headlights shed light on the scene. They had her, and were shoving her into the backseat of the Mustang.

Do I save Kelley? How could I?

Then the door between the kitchen and garage opened. Aurora stood on the top step blindfolded by a strip of black duct tape, and silenced by another strip across her mouth. Rayjohn towered over her, and pushed her down the steps. He seemed to press a button on a remote, and the side car came out of the Spider's body near me.

"OK, old woman! We're taking a little ride. I wanna know how this thing works. Maybe we can make a little money with it!"

I hid behind a dumpster. He pushed her around the back of the garage to the sidecar, shoved her in, and put the seatbelt around her. I knew there was a place behind her seat where she stored groceries and stuff. While Rayjohn was in the cockpit trying to figure out the Spider's controls, I fit myself in. Just room enough. I leaned over and whispered in her ear, "I'm behind you." She gave me a thumbs up, and I slid back down into the space.

Could this no brain bully actually control the Spider?

He was leafing through a booklet that might have been a driver's manual. He pressed some keys on the remote, and we started to move down the driveway. He steered the Spider behind the Mustang which had already pulled away from the curb. Mick drove the Mustang out of the cul-de-sac onto Watson Drive as we followed close behind.

Mick led us out of the quiet subdivision streets and through the town, shut down for the night. We picked up speed and merged onto the interstate. He began leading us on a high speed chase, weaving in and out of eighteen wheelers doing at least 75 mph. I was crunched over in the storage bin behind Aurora. Her head was bent over as it was when she prayed. We must have hit 90 mph. Where were the cops?

I remembered the scripture Aurora wrote on my cast. Psalm 27:1,2 "The Lord is my light and my salvation. Whom shall I fear? The Lord is the stronghold of my life. Of whom should I be afraid?" These words of King David came to my mind as the Spider rounded a sharp curve.

I looked up quickly and saw that Rayjohn was tail-gating the Mustang. We suddenly pulled into the left lane behind it. Mick swerved to get out of the way of an eighteen wheeler that was passing very close to him. We were on a sharp curve in the road, and the Mustang veered onto the shoulder and stopped.

Aurora had removed the tape from her mouth and whispered, "It's time, Davy. Don't be afraid."

I raised my head and saw she had another remote in her

hand. She punched in numbers and letters on the keyboard. Then, a loud rushing of wind was all around us. A strong force hit us in our chests, pushing us way back in our seats like astronauts taking off in a rocket. Outside, pearly strings of gooey material oozed from every pore of the Spider's skin. It formed a canopy around us, and I felt it lifting us off the road onto the grassy shoulder.

The Spider came to a sudden stop. In the cockpit, Rayjohn had been pressing every button on the remote to get the Spider to do something. He said a cuss word and his head fell forward hitting the steering wheel. He looked unconscious.

Aurora gently removed the duct tape blindfold. She turned to me, smiled, and held up a small remote. "Rayjohn grabbed the TV remote by mistake. I've been guiding us all along with the real one."

We heard sirens and saw flashing lights! Emergency cars and trucks parked around us. Dark figures circled the Spider outside the web.

"There's people in there, alive, I hope. We need some sharp cutting blades to get through this web. Never seen anything like this before! Anybody got a chain saw?"

"Hang in there, folks. There's an ambulance waiting." I recognized the voice of Detective Sergeant Peterson.

I shouted, "There is someone who may be unconscious. Two of us are OK, though. My sister is in the Mustang. Please get her out first. The other guys are kidnappers!"

Three men cut through the web with wire cutters until they reached the sidecar, and a young paramedic lifted Aurora gently from the seat. Rayjohn was bleeding but conscious when paramedics got him into to an ambulance.

Aurora, Kelley, and I explained the situation to Sgt. Peterson, while two other policemen handcuffed Mick and Jackson and led them to the backseat of Sgt. Peterson's police car.

Someone called a tow truck to get the Spider back to Aurora's garage. We rode to Aurora's in another police car in time to welcome the Spider back home. He was safe and sound once the web dried up and fell on the garage floor.

Doug was in the kitchen with duct tape around his muzzle. The glue stuck to his hair, and he whimpered in pain when I gently peeled it off.

"I know how you feel, Doug," Aurora petted him. "The hooligans did it to me,. too." Her skin was red around her eyes and mouth. She sat down at the table and put her head down on her arms.

I called Mom from Aurora's phone. She was worried. It was late and I wasn't home. I was too tired to tell the whole story, but she was happy we were all safe.

Kelley made some hot chocolate. We stayed together in the kitchen, too tired to move. We needed to tell our stories about the day's events over and over.

There were two questions that puzzled me about the remote Aurora said she used to control the Spider. I needed answers.

"Aurora, how did Rayjohn get his hands on the Spider remote?"

"Ha, ha. It was on the kitchen counter. I always keep the TV remote in the same place so I can watch the news while I eat dinner. The TV is on the wall."

"How come he thought he had the Spider remote?" A logical question!

"He asked me where it was and I pointed to it. Mind you, they duct taped my mouth shut. I always keep the Spider remote close to me. Fortunately, I had it in my pants pocket. I had time to take it out and hide it under my shirt before he belted me into the sidecar."

"Yeah, that was lucky! But you were blindfolded on the whole ride, right?"

"So?"

"So how could you see to control the remote?"

"I haven't trained you to drive the Spider. I must do that soon." She pulled the remote out of her pants pocket and placed it in front of me on the table.

"My Louis designed this to have many features. If I touch the green button, the person with the remote controls the speed, direction and all functions of the Spider. You just have to know what buttons to press."

"That's great, but your eyes were covered in tape. How could you see out the windshield?"

"Oh ye of little faith!" She pointed to a red button next to the green one. "Press this button and you are free to take a nap, read a book, whatever. The Spider is smart enough to control itself, if you let it. And it is probably a better driver than any of us."

"Oh, I should have guessed." I could feel myself drifting off to sleep. My eyes were heavy.

Finally, Aurora whispered a short prayer before we fell asleep, heads down on the table.

"This was God's work, you know. He got us through this. Thank you, Lord."

36
CHAPTER

SERVING UP JUSTICE

A WEEK LATER we sat around a conference table at police headquarters: me, Kelley, Mom, Dad, Aurora, Corey, his mother Suzanna, Rayjohn, Mick and his mother, Jackson and his dad. Sgt.Peterson sat at the head of the table with Rayjohn to his right. Mick and Jackson faced Rayjohn across the table.

"Strange case. I've been trying to connect the dots." Sgt. Peterson had also interviewed Aurora in the food poisoning case.

"First of all, how are you all connected to the crime, and which crime? I thought the apple tart case was a done deal. Ms. Aurora, sorry to put you through another investigation. So I'll let you go first. What is going on here?"

He focused on her large brown eyes now outlined in a dark eye liner and blue eye shadow. She blinked a few times, and her red lips curled up into a half smile.

"The three young men sitting next to you," she pointed a long

David, the Big D, and the Playground Goliath

red fingernail at Rayjohn, Mick, and Jackson, "those hooligans tried to kidnap Kelley and me. They broke into my house; they duct taped the dog; and they duct taped my mouth and eyes. The leader of the pack pushed me into the sidecar of my Spider and took me on a dangerous ride. Thank goodness David had snuck into the space behind me.

These other two hooligans kidnapped Kelley and put her in the red Mustang. There was no duct tape involved there. I did not have the same kindness shown to me, an elderly woman."

"And David Kingston, you're up next."

I told my side of the story, just the facts and not the feelings about my father and the Mafia.

"You went to your father's house to give Kelley a birthday present from your mom, right?"

"Yes, Sir."

"There was a big party going on. How did your sister seem when you first saw her?"

"She was drunk. And she was angry."

"Angry at who?"

"At Rayjohn. She threw a piece of birthday cake in his face. And he called her the 'b' word, you know."

The smirk on Rayjohn's face was noted by everyone.

"And what happened next?"

"I sprayed lavender perfume in his eyes, a whole bottle. He couldn't see for a while so we had time to run."

"Well done, David. Quick thinking! You must be proud of your kid," he nodded at my dad who looked down at the table.

"Mr. Kingston, are you also Kelley's father?"

Dad looked up and smiled.

"Yes I'm her father."

"Was the party at your house, sir?"

"Yes. I left Rayjohn in charge. He is old enough."

"I see. And where were you?"

Dad's face turned deep red, and from across the table I could smell his sweat. "I was with Suzanne," he mumbled, "at her place, barbecuing. She invited me to dinner."

Mom gasped. Kelley put her arms around Mom's shoulder, whispered in her ear, and led her out of the room.

Detective Sgt. Peterson focused on Rayjohn.

"Mr. Roybell, may I see your driver's license?"

His hand trembled as he stood for a second, and took his wallet out of the back pocket of his jeans. He opened the beat up leather wallet and pulled out a card with his photo on the right corner. He slid it on the table to the detective.

"Hmm. According to this, you are 19 years old, an adult in my eyes, and also in the eyes of the court. Tell me, what activities took place at the party? And what illegal substances were present in that house?"

"Just kids having fun, sir, dancing, eating, drinking."

Detective Peterson tapped his pen on the table. "Drinking? What were your guests drinking?"

"Apple cider," he said.

I interrupted. "He's lying, sir."

"Go ahead, Davy."

"They were drinking Apple Beer. My sister was drunk."

"Any smoking going on, Davy?"

"The house smelled of it. It was the stuff Rayjohn sells to kids at school."

"Rayjohn Roybell, do you attend school?" he asked.

"No. What do I need school for? I have a job. I manage Hunger Heights Luxury Apartments for my dad. Don't need no education."

"Hmm," Sgt. Peterson looked at Suzanne next.

"And you, ma'am, are Mr. Kingston's girl friend?"

"Yes," she smiled. " We are engaged. We plan to get married when his divorce is final. And for your information, Rayjohn is my nephew, and he is innocent! And that woman over there, that evil old woman…" She stood up and pointed at Aurora. "She is the one you should be arresting. She is a menace! That big black ugly thing she drives is scaring everyone in the neighborhood. Don't forget the poison apple tarts she sold at the game."

"Ma'am, I'm just looking at the facts of this case. And for the record, Ms. Aurora is no more a menace to society than you are. Aurora Gardner is a fine woman of faith. We go to the same church. The whole congregation would stand behind her."

Corey popped up from his seat. "If my mom says she's a menace, she is a menace!"

"And you must be the little genius. The one who sprinkled traces of pesticide on the peeled apples. Didn't take the police lab and middle school teacher long to figure that out. Combined with Davy's and Aurora's statements, you came up as the only suspect. Good thing no one got seriously sick, and no one filed charges. Good thing for you that you're not old enough to stand trial."

Crocodile tears poured out of Corey's eyes. Suzanne shot a cold look at the Detective.

"I have some recommendations to make about this case. Corey, you are a minor and will not face a penalty. However, I believe that one full year of counseling, once a week, would be in order here. The court will be in touch with your school counselor."

He nodded to Suzanna and my dad. "As for you two, I will also recommend that the judge order parenting classes, since you will be parenting together. That is, assuming you get married. Mr. Kingston, you are negligent for allowing a teenage party with beer and other illegal stuff in your house. You put your own daughter in danger."

Dad glared at Rayjohn who glared back at him with a half smile.

Mick and Jackson squirmed.

"Stop fidgeting. Stand up like real men. Look David and Ms Aurora in the eyes and apologize."

The three stood up, made quick eye contact with us, and mumbled, "Sorry."

"Can we go now?" Rayjohn stared unflinchingly at Sgt. Peterson.

"Sit down!" he commanded. "I cannot pass sentences on you. That is for the judge. There will be a court hearing in three days to determine if you should face trial.

Rayjohn Roybell, since you are an adult and charges against you are more serious, you will remain here in the jail until the hearing. Mick and Jackson can leave with their parents. Meeting adjourned."

I stood and waited as an officer handcuffed Rayjohn, head bent, still smirking. He was hunched over between two police officers. He didn't look so big to me then. As they opened a side door leading to the jail cells, Rayjohn turned his head toward me. An icy stare, a whisper, "I'll get you for this, Davy!"

"For God did not give me a spirit of fear but of power, love, and self control." 2Timothy :1-7 Another scripture I learned from Aurora that popped into my head when we locked eyes.

Then he faced forward and disappeared. The heavy metal door clanged shut.

37
CHAPTER

A TALE OF TWO DAVIDS

AURORA AND I sat at the kitchen table. I was taking a break from weeding the vegetable garden. She had made an icy cold pitcher of lemonade to accompany fresh baked croissants.

"Aurora, did you name your son after David in the Bible?"

We had been discussing the early chapters of 1 Samuel when Saul became Israel's first King. It seemed that Saul first met David in the Valley of Elah, when young David killed the giant Goliath.

"Oui." We could have chosen many names from the Bible: Abraham, Noah, or Jonathan from the Old Testament; Peter or John from the New Testament. We picked David because God gave him so many talents, yet he was humble. He loved God and obeyed Him."

"I have been reading more about him. He was pretty cool, but you always say that no one is perfect. Everyone sins. Did David ever sin?"

"Of course. Only one man never sinned. You will be meeting him as you read and study His book."

"That must be Jesus!"

"Yes. You will find him soon enough. Would you like another croissant? Try some of my raspberry jam, Davy."

"Sure, and more lemonade, please. Thank you. You said the name Jonathan. I have a Jewish friend named Jonathan. I went to his Bar Mitzvah last year."

She looked up from the rim of her coffee cup and winked.

"Jonathan was David's best friend. He also happened to be King Saul's oldest son who would one day inherit the throne of Israel."

"So when Saul died, Jonathan would be King?"

"Things don't always happen according to the plans of men," she laughed.

"I guess not. I never thought my mom and dad would get divorced. So, how did David and Jonathan become besties?"

"You will have to read about it in 1 Samuel 19-21. But I will tell you that David became part of Saul's household. And for a long while King Saul loved him like a son."

"Wouldn't that make Jonathan jealous?"

"No. Jonathan and David became close friends. I think Jonathan admired David. It was David's musical talent that brought him to the King. All of Saul's family liked listening to David's songs. He was like a rock star. He wrote poems called Psalms which he set to music, and he sang them."

"Maybe he and Jonathan sang together."

"Maybe they did. But I know they liked to shoot bows and arrows. They both were good at archery."

I was thinking of my new best friend, Bart, and how much we loved shooting baskets together.

"So, I guess David and Jonathan were forever friends?"

"Well, as the saying goes, nothing lasts forever," she shrugged.

"Yeah, I'm not as friendly with Buddy anymore since he has a girlfriend who happens to be Kelley. No time for me anymore."

"David also served in Saul's army. He was a leader who won many battles and became popular. The people began to sing this song, 'Saul has slain his thousands, and David has slain his tens of thousands.'"(1Samuel 21:11)

"Wow, that must have made Saul mad and jealous," I said.

"Yes. So mad that he planned to kill David. And you remember that God was mad at Saul. God no longer supported him because Saul had disobeyed his commands."

"He switched his support to David. Samuel had already anointed him with oil, right?"

She laughed and clapped her hands, "You are learning, David!"

"But what about Jonathan? Wasn't he supposed to be the next King? And can I please have a macaroon?"

She passed me a plate filled with colorful coconut cookies. I picked one dipped in chocolate.

"Jonathan knew about his father's plan. But Jonathan loved David, and he knew that David would be a better King than his father, and perhaps a better King than himself. He warned David so that he could escape and hide out in the desert."

"I know David finally becomes King, but what about Jonathan? Does David make him an assistant king or something? Were they still friends?"

"Keep reading. You will see."

"Jonathan had David's back, but did David have Jonathan's back?"

Aurora gathered the dishes, walked toward the kitchen sink, and looked over her shoulder at me. "That, you will also find out."

38
CHAPTER

BEGINNINGS

I WILL BE starting high school in two weeks. Will I meet more playground Goliaths? Probably. But this year I have Bart, and we have each other's back. I have Doug back in my life too thanks to my job with Aurora. And I have good friends I never would have met if it hadn't been for the Big D.

I have gained 20 pounds and three feet of height. Suddenly I am tall and thin. Mom complains about the grocery bill because I eat like there's no tomorrow. I don't even sound like my old puny self. My voice is deeper and steadier, so I'm beginning to talk and walk like a man.

I'm trying out for basketball when school starts, and getting in shape lifting weights with Tony and Bart. I go to a teen Bible study at Aurora's church, and plan to join the science club at school. I read everything I can about spiders and mechanics. And I read the Bible every night, especially First and Second Samuel. I want to know more about David, Israel's greatest

King. But I want to know more about Jesus Christ, and David will lead me to Him.

Tony, Bart, and I are still trying to figure out the mysteries behind Louis Gardner's Spider. Tony has probed every inch of the Spider and is convinced it is a hybrid, a unique combination of biology and technology. And no, it doesn't run on human blood. Genuine blue spider blood runs through its veins.

I do not see my dad. We both need space from each other. Kelley and I are tight, and she is back at Hunger Heights Apartments with Mom and me. Mom is smoking less, and has not had beer for months. She is working more hours at Food Circus and is being considered for management training. We go to Aurora's Church every Sunday. We are eating better, and of course, we say grace before every meal.

Rayjohn is spending time at a youth rehab farm somewhere in Colorado. His father is a big wig with connections. So I doubt that he is suffering too much. I hope he gets roughed around by the bullies, like I did. Maybe he will change. I heard there are Bible classes for prisoners. I am praying for him.

Corey's school counselor suggested he do twenty hours of public service as part of his therapy. Every Saturday morning he is at the City Animal Shelter. He walks the dogs and cleans out their cages. I visited him once. He seemed glad to see me.

He said he doesn't much like picking up poop, but loves walking and playing with the dogs, especially a hyper-active black Chihuahua named Pippa. "I have dibs on adopting her when I'm done serving my time. My mom says that's OK if it keeps me out of trouble."

Of course, I still work for Aurora on Saturdays. She is selling her tarts at Maximus and Son Mechanical Repairs. Mom, Kelley, and I help with baking. I do odd jobs on the property, and I stay away from the shed because now I know what's inside. It is not full of cages for lost kids or anything illegal, I don't think. Another story!

The further I get from it, the smaller the Big D becomes. But I hate divorce. God hates divorce, too. Men and women invented divorce, not God. Divorce hurt my mom and my dad too, I suppose. But Kelley and me, it hurt us so, so bad, even now.

God turns bad into good if you let Him work in you. I want to let Him in. I want to do life God's way.

Aurora says I will sin and make mistakes. God knows I will, but the God I am learning about day by day loves me. He is forgiving. So I must forgive, too, even Rayjohn, even my dad. And for that I need to know Jesus who is even greater than the Bible David. I can't wait to meet him, although Aurora says I already have.

ACKNOWLEDGEMENTS

David, the Big D, and the Playground Goliath is a product of the COVID, like many other books. I do not wish to thank the COVID for the boredom that inspired me to get back to writing. I want to thank the Lord for keeping my family and me safe and healthy through it all. I thank my good friend Kay Strait for the fun we had brainstorming the concept. We watched a Master Class tutorial by R.L Stine, author of the Goosebumps series. Then we generated some ideas about characters and conveying a Christian message throughout the work. We edited the book together. Without her collaboration, encouragement, love of the Lord, and sense of humor, this book would not exist.

Thanks to the Rio Rancho Church of Christ, the ministers through the years, and especially the Church itself, the people who have inspired me with their faith, fellowship, and love. Thanks to Lani who's faith and love of the Lord was more contagious then COVID. Thanks to my brother Cliff and my sister-in-law Cheryl. Thanks to Herman, my dad. I was blessed to have you as my father and role model.

I thank the many people who have influenced me and guided me on my Christian journey. I especially thank my late husband Kenneth Gossett who inspired me the most to grow in my faith, and to love the Word. I love you, Ken, and I miss you every day.

I thank my daughters Eve and Anne, and four grandchildren: Maddie, Luke, Alex, and Josh. I love you all. Luke, Alex, and Josh, there is a little bit of each of you in Davy.

This book is for you and because of you. Bullies will be at every stage of your lives. As you read and study the Bible, you will learn that you were not created to be victims. That is not God's plan for us. We are all meant to be conquerors through Jesus Christ.

Printed in the United States
by Baker & Taylor Publisher Services